Holy Hilarity, Joy for the Soul

~

Humorous Stories

William W. Moore

JEC PUBLISHING COMPANY
2049 E. Cherry Street, Suite 100
Springfield, Missouri 65802
(800) 313-5121
www.jecpubco.com

Copyright © 2009 by William W. Moore

Library of Congress Control Number: 2009937908

ISBN: 978-0-9824801-5-1

Author: William W. Moore

Cover Design by: Harold Scherler

Prepared for Publishing by: JE Cornwell and Tom Dease

Proofed and Edited by: Pam Eddings

Printed in Canada

All rights reserved.
This publication; *Holy Hilarity: Joy for the Soul,* its content and cover are the property of William W. Moore. This book or parts thereof, may not be reproduced in any form without permission from William W. Moore or JEC Publishing Company; exceptions are made for printed reviews and advertising and marketing excerpts.

This book is dedicated to the Glory of God

*I hope this book brings a little laughter your way.
Thus, my prayer for you is that you may rejoice in the Lord
always, knowing that "goodness and mercy shall follow you"
– pursue you, and time-and-again catch up with you – and
that you "shall dwell in the House of the Lord for ever!"
(Philippians 4:4-5a & Psalm 23:4 & 6)
Amen!*

*In honor of Benjamin William Moore &
Bethany Ann Moore, our precious grandchildren
who keep me laughing!*

*I am grateful to my sister, Marilyn Amelia Moore,
for her help in getting the manuscript
ready for the publisher.*

The translation used in the course of this book is from the Revised Standard Version of the Bible.

Introduction

This book is the result of 40 years of preaching the Gospel. In these pages you will find stories I have gleaned, and experiences I have had, that I found to be humorous.

As Christians we take ourselves, and life far too seriously! We fail to see the joys God places about us daily, like Easter eggs for His children to find, i.e. the baby robin in the nest, the flower sprouting forth with its first bloom, the snowflake falling quietly to the ground. Ours is a great God, a loving Parent, and sometimes a Comedian.

Over these years I have interjected humor in my sermons. Humor has a way of putting people at ease, and making them ready to listen. It breaks down barriers between the speaker and hearers. It puts the speaker on the same level with those who listen. It is a good tool – a gift God has given us. Thus, it is Holy Hilarity!

I did *not* use all of the humor in this book in sermons. Some stories are included simply for your enjoyment. However, the vast majority I did use, and feel they would be appropriate for Sunday School teachers, preachers, public speakers, or for personal amusement.

Years ago, I read a book, the title and author of which I have forgotten, that helped shape my presentation of humor. The author noted that just as you need a "punch line," so also you need a "punch word." Both should come at the end of the funny story you are telling. If you can, the punch word should be the *last* word, or very near to the last word in the story. This gives the telling greater effect. I have tried to practice this in all the humorous tales in this book.

In the mid 1960s, I read a book entitled: "The Humor of Christ" by Dr. Elton Trueblood. I had grown up with the realization that God was a God of judgment primarily, but also One of love – but a God who *laughs*? It sounded sacrilegious! Through Trueblood's book I began to see this side of our Lord.

Jesus often used hyperbole – exaggeration – to make a point. He used it to get persons to drop their defenses, hear, and remember. The following are a few examples:

1. To the critic he said: "Take the log out of your own eye, then you will see clearly how to remove the speck in your brother's eye!" (Matthew 7:3) Jesus envisioned a man having a log hanging out of his eye, saying to another: "Hey, buddy, you have a speck in your eye. Let me show you how to get that out!" We do not know if the critics, to whom He was speaking, got the message, but others did, and, I am sure, laughed!

2. Jesus said: "Do not be anxious for tomorrow, for tomorrow will be anxious for itself. Let today's own trouble be sufficient for today (Matthew 6:34)." Our Lord must have smiled as He thought of the poor worrier saying to himself: "You know, I don't have enough to worry about, so I am going to consider all the bad things that could happen tomorrow, and worry about them." Again, the people must have chuckled, but got the point!

3. Finally, He said, "It is easier for a camel to go through the eye of a needle, than for a rich man to enter the kingdom of God (Luke 18:25)." We can debate the nature of the "needle" to which Jesus is referring. Some Bible scholars believe Jesus was referring to a very small, low door through the fortress or city wall. Others would see it as a reference to a tool for sewing. In either case you can see how funny the imagery is. Imagine a camel attempting to get both humps through the opening! Or think of the rich man with a large derriere trying to get through, and hanging up in a most embarrassing way! Through this humor Jesus got His message across to the rich ruler, who could not find it within himself to sell all and follow (verse 22).

Dr. Trueblood gave many more illustrations of our Lord's use of humor. But I shall let these three examples suffice.

But, BEWARE! The vast majority of congregants do not find Jesus' humor funny. Sorry, Lord! Today His humor falls flat! For we Christians, including pastors, cannot imagine a laughing Jesus – one who enjoyed a funny analogy – a good joke – a belly laugh, if you will! So, if you are doing a humorous presentation, stay away from the humor of Jesus, for it will be greeted with silence! We know that "Jesus wept" (John 11:35), but have a hard time imagining that Jesus was the "life of the party" who laughed too!

Now humor can be destructive! This is true in two ways. First, it can be used to make light of circumstances, rather than showing true feelings. Those who use it in this way, carefully build a wall around themselves to prevent anyone from coming in.

Second, there are those who use humor to put others down. They try to leave the appearance of "kidding," but the end result is very hurtful.

These two forms of humor are not what Jesus used, and are not the sort which I use here.

This book contains primarily "black humor" – i.e. humor that makes light of life's trials, and our human foibles. It is humor that may humble us, but not humiliate us. It carries a message and a laugh. Who else but followers of the risen Christ could possibly laugh in a world like this?

The great Martin Luther, while struggling with mental depression and the threat of assassination, wrote, "For though this world with devils filled should threaten to undo us. We will not fear, for God has willed his truth to triumph through us!" You can readily hear the note of JOY in this great hymn! ("A Mighty Fortress is Our God")

Before we go further, I must address the subject of Christian joy. Christian joy is *not* lighthearted gaiety! It is not the cheap, saintly smile that seems artificial, because it is. It is not what is commonly hawked as "believe in the Lord, and you will have wealth, health, and happiness forevermore! " Christians and secular persons face many troubles in life just like our Lord and the apostle Paul did. Thus, this Joy is based on an inner relationship with the risen Christ rather than outward circumstances. It was only on this basis that the apostle could write: "Rejoice in the Lord always; again I will say, Rejoice!" (Philippians 4:4) even while wishing that he could die, and be with the Lord! (Philippians 1:21-23)

Christian joy is the knowledge, and inner assurance, that we stand on the Rock! It is peace! It is an inner sense that: "even though I walk through the valley of the shadow of death, I will fear no evil for thou art with me! (Psalm 23:4). And time-and-time again it breaks forth in exuberant song!

How do we "get" this Joy? It is not something that we "get," but something that is *given* to the one who prays with thanksgiving. (Philippians 4:4-7) That's it! For through prayer we come to realize the dependability of our great God!

So, I hope this book will give you a few laughs, and while doing so, that it will lift your spirit up into the Presence of the Christ of Joy. After all it is Holy Hilarity: Joy for the Soul!

****

1. Humbling Experiences

Willsie Martin tells of a time when he was pastor of the Wilshire Boulevard Church in Los Angeles. The church, like many from that era, had a number of steps to climb to get into the sanctuary. He had been at the church just a few weeks when one Sunday, as he parked the car, he saw an elderly woman starting her ascent. He hurriedly caught up with her. She took him by the arm saying: "Thank you, young man!" When they arrived at the landing she turned to him and said, "Sir, do you know who is preaching today?" He smiled, squared his shoulders, and stuck out his chest as he announced: "Why, Willsie Martin!" With that the woman said: "Sir, do you mind helping back down the steps?"

(**Message:** About the time we get to feeling overly proud of ourselves, God has a way of humbling us.)

*****

2. Pride

A wealthy woman knew very little about her family history. So she hired a renowned author and researcher to trace her roots. He agreed, with the stipulation that he be free to put in print whatever he discovered. She consented, and the author began his work.

A month later he reported that he had already found a skeleton in the closet! Her great grandfather had been convicted of first degree murder, and was electrocuted in Sing Sing Prison.

She was aghast! She had told friends in her high society circles of her upcoming book of family history, but she could not let this out! Yet, she remembered the contract she had with her writer. So she pleaded: "Please do whatever you can to make this look as good as possible!"

She was delighted when a week later she read: "Her paternal great grandfather, George Buckley, occupied the chair of applied electricity in one of our nation's leading institutions. He was very attached to his position, and literally died in the harness."

(**Application:** "Be sure your sin will find you out!" Numbers 32:23b)

*****

3. Time to Wake!
A church in Connecticut was having worship when an elderly gentleman fainted. Someone ran and called "911." The paramedics arrived, and carted out twenty people before they found the right one.

The Canadian railroad advertised: "200 sleepers for a trans-Canada trip of a lifetime!" A pastor in Iowa offered his entire congregation!
(**Challenge:** "Awake O sleeper, and arise from the dead, and Christ shall give you light" Ephesians 5:14)

*****

4. Deadly Distractions
A man in Dallas was preparing to catch the bus for Beaumont. It was going to be an hour before the bus arrived, so he looked for someway to pass the time. He spotted a scale that advertised: "50 cents to tell all about you!" He thought it a little high for just finding out his weight, but decided to try it. He dropped a half dollar into the scales and stepped on. A card popped out which read: "You have blonde hair, blue eyes and weigh 165 pounds." The gentleman could not believe it! The machine was right! But what if it told everyone that? Intrigued he put in another 50 cents. Stepped on the scale. Out popped a card: "You have blonde hair, blue eyes; you weigh 165 pounds, and are waiting for a bus for Beaumont." Now this was totally unbelievable!

He still had a little over thirty minutes, so he decided to go down to a novelty store a block away. There he bought a mask, a black wig, and a scarf to go around his neck. He had one half dollar left, so he dropped it in the slot. Stepped on the scale. Out popped the card which read: You STILL have blonde hair, blue eyes, and weigh 165 pounds, and now you have fooled around and missed that bus to Beaumont!"
(Story told by The Reverend Dr. Robert Arbaugh. **Message:** There are many distractions in life that get us off course!)

*****

5. Humility
At the close of the service an elderly woman made her way to the door. She shook my hand, and then she gushed: "Brother Moore, I had to take

two pain pills to come and hear you preach this morning."
     (**Message:** You can count on God's "saints" to keep you humble.)

*****

6. Humanity's Answers
James Johnson, a chicken farmer who lived way down in the Ozarks, began losing chickens. He wrote to the County Agent about his dilemma: "Dear Sir, something is wrong with my chickens. Every morning I go out to the hen house, and find two or three of them lying cold and stiff on the ground. Can you tell me what is the matter?" By return mail the agent replied: "Dear Mr. Johnson, your chickens are DEAD!"
     (Story from a file of the Agriculture Department – **Message:** Too many times we miss the obvious!)

*****

7. Understanding or Beyond Description
Someone once asked Albert Einstein to explain his famous theory of relativity in simple words. The noted scientist smiled and responded: "I am sorry I cannot do that. But if you will come to my home at Princeton, I will play it for you on my violin!"
     (**Application:** There are things of the Spirit that must be experienced to understand! – Romans 8:26)

*****

8. Praying to Whom?
Dr. James McCosh, one time president of Princeton, was leading the chapel service one morning. As he was praying a closing prayer, he remembered an announcement he was supposed to have made for a professor of a class in German. Realizing that as soon as he said, "Amen" the students would bolt for the door, he added: "And Lord bless the Senior German Class, which meets this morning at 10:00 instead of the usual 11:00. Amen."

Someone once described an elaborate prayer spoken before an elite Boston congregation as "the most eloquent prayer ever offered to a Boston audience."

    (**Message:** To WHOM are you praying? See: Matthew 6:7)

*****

9. Nature of Prayer
Years ago in the Saturday Review there was a cartoon by William Hoest. It depicted a pajama clad youngster ready for bed, who called out: "I'm going to say my prayers. Anyone want anything?"

    (**Message:** Far and away our greatest need is God!)

*****

10. Consequences
In the days when a pastor would visit door-to-door, Reverend Mitchell was making his rounds. It was a beautiful Spring day. He walked up the sidewalk to a two storied house. Looking through the screen door, he noticed the door was standing open. He knocked, and heard someone inside call out: "Come in. Come in!"

Hesitantly he accepted the invitation by opening the screen door, and stepping in. Again he heard: "Come in. Come in!" So he followed the sound into the kitchen. As he entered the room, a large German Shepherd lunged at him from under the table, pinning him to the wall. With a paw on each shoulder, his snarling teeth were but inches from his face. Then he heard it again: "Come in – come in!" He turned his eyes toward the voice and saw the family's parrot in its cage over in the corner. With that the preacher snarled: "You stupid bird! Can't you say anything else?" With that the parrot cried: "Sic–im – sic-im!"

    (**Application:** There are unexpected troubles in life most of which are of our own making!)

*****

11. Courage
A couple was on vacation when they had to make an emergency stop at a dentist's office. The wife approached the dentist declaring: "We are on

a trip, and do not have a lot of time. I'd like for you to pull a tooth. Do not take time for any anesthetic. Just pull the tooth!" Impressed by the woman's courage, the dentist asked: "Which tooth is it?" She turned, grabbed her husband and said: "Show him your tooth, dear!"

(**Message:** It is easy for us to be brave when we have nothing invested.)

*****

12. Gospel as Motivator
It is said that Philosopher, John Dewey, was walking along with his young son one cold rainy day. While Dewey stopped to visit with a neighbor, his young son found a large puddle and began splashing in it. The friend said: "John, you had better get that boy out of the water or he will surely get pneumonia!" "I know," said the philosopher, "but I am trying to think of a way to make him WANT to get out of the water."

(My father was not a philosopher, but *he* knew how to make me *want* to get out of the water! It was called "Applied Psychology!" **Message:** Unlike laws and "thou shall nots," the Gospel makes us WANT to live for Him!)

*****

13. Our God of Possibilities
A young mother asked her son what he learned in Sunday School. He said, "We learned about a time long ago when God sent Moses behind the enemy's lines to rescue the Israelites in Egypt. As they were making their escape, Moses called on the engineers to build a pontoon bridge across the sea. Hardly had they made it across when the Egyptian soldiers tried to cross. Moses radioed for fighters to come. They swept down and blew up the bridge, sending all the Egyptians into the sea where they drowned!"

"Now Billy!" his mother scolded, "that is *not* the way the story goes!" "Well, not exactly," replied Billy, "but if I told it, the way Mrs. Broom told it, you would *never* believe it!"

(**Message:** Ours is a God of unimaginable possibilities -- a God who does miracles in our time!)

*****

14. Things are not what they seem
A Methodist coed invited her roommate home for the weekend. On Sunday they went to the local Methodist Church. The roommate, who was a Roman Catholic (now a Roaming Catholic) had never attended a Protestant Church. It was all going to be new to her. As they entered the sanctuary, she pecked the Methodist on the shoulder and whispered: "Don't you genuflect as you enter?" "No, we just go to our seats." She followed. Again she whispered: "Why is your cross empty?" The Methodist responded: "Our cross reminds us of the risen Savior." There were other questions. Finally the pastor entered, and placed his Bible on the pulpit. Then he took off his watch and laid it beside the Bible. The Catholic coed asked: "What does that mean?" Her friend replied: "It doesn't mean a darn thing!"

(**Message:** Things are not always what they seem to be especially in the eyes of worshippers!)

*****

15. Surprises – or – Best laid plans fall short!
Back during the Great Depression of the 1930s, Momma and Poppa lived on a farm down in the Ozarks. They had no electricity, no phone, no car, nor little else that we would consider essentials today. Poppa worked hard to "make ends meet," for times were "hard."

Poppa had only one pair of bib overalls that had been patched several times. Time after time Momma would say to him: "Dad," for that is what she called him, "why don't ye git ye some new overalls when ye go to town." But Poppa did not think the family could afford such a luxury.

One day it was time to go to town and sell a load of corn that he had managed to raise that year. So, as he left, Momma gave her familiar admonition about his overalls. He hooked the horse to the wagon piled with corn. When he got to town he went by the mill and sold his corn. It brought more than he thought it would, so he bought a 25 pound bag of flour, and one of sugar. Also, he could buy some new clothes and surprise Momma when he got back home. So, he went by the clothing store. He told the clerk that he wanted to purchase a brand new pair of Big Ben overalls size 28" X 32". She got them. He started to pay, but realized he would still have money left, so decided to get a new plaid flannel shirt, underwear, and socks. He was fixed! He would certainly surprise Momma now! He paid the clerk. She put all of his purchases in a brown paper bag. He put it under his arm and went out to his waiting horse and wagon. He climbed up onto the seat, and put the bag behind him in the floor. After making one more stop, he mounted his wagon again, and left for home at a gallop. He would truly surprise Momma this time!

He got out there in the bottom land by the river where the one lonely bridge crossed. He pulled the horse up to a girder, and tied the steed there. He looked both directions, and no one was in sight either way. So, he took off that old pair of worn out overalls, and gave them a mighty pitch into the swirling water below. He did the same with his tattered shirt, socks, and underwear. Then he reached back for the sack of new clothes…. It was not there! He looked, and the clothes were no where to be found! Finally he said to himself: "Well, I'll jist go home and surprise Momma anyway!"
      (**Application:** The best laid plans of humanity always fall short! – Paraphrased from "To a Mouse" by Robert Frost)

*****

16. Christianity Lite – or – Conversion
The story is told of an Episcopalian man who lived in a neighborhood of predominately Roman Catholics. It was back in the days when Catholics were expected to eat fish on Fridays. It seemed like every Friday evening, from early March on through September, the Episcopalian would uncover his grill on the patio, light it, then disappear inside the house. He would reappear with a platter of the most delectable steaks you ever saw! Carefully placing them on the grill, they would begin to sizzle. The smoke would rise, and the aroma would waft its way around the neighborhood, titillating the senses.

Finally, his Catholic neighbors had had all they could take! They called a neighborhood meeting, minus the Episcopalian, to consider their problem. Someone came up with the solution of converting him to Catholicism. The rest quickly agreed. Soon they were putting their best efforts into being effective witnesses to their faith.

Sure enough the day came when the man was converted. The priest intoned over the kneeling man: "Born an Episcopalian. Raised an Episcopalian. Now you are a Catholic!" His Catholic neighbors breathed a big sigh of relief!

But they could not help but wonder if it "took." For come Friday they were all peeking out their windows as the new convert fired up his grill. He disappeared into his house. Eventually he came out with what they assumed would be fish, but it was more steaks! They could not believe it! He placed the steaks on the grill, and as they began to sizzle, he was heard to chant: "Born a beef. Raised a beef. – Now you're a FISH!"

(**Message:** We like to pick and choose the parts of Christianity that meet our needs, and desires.)

*****

17. Doctrinal Teachings
A Sunday School teacher was trying to explain the nature of the Trinity. She said: "The Trinity is like an egg. It has a yoke, a white, and a shell. Three parts, one egg." To demonstrate, she, with great drama, held high an egg she had brought from home. Broke it into a bowl, and out came a – double yoke!

(**Message:** We always fall short when we try to explain God. – See: Romans 16:25; Ephesians 3:3-9)

*****

18. On Giving…
A gentleman from New York City traveled to Maine to visit his country cousin, Tom Mason, who had a mink farm. At any given time he had four to six dozen mink to harvest for their valuable pelts. Tom took him on a tour of the pens where the mink were fed and cared for. His city cousin hung on every word. Wanting to make some intelligent conversation, he asked: "Say, Tom, how often do you skin these mink?" Not wanting to embarrass him, Tom replied: "Only once a year. Anymore often than that makes them awfully nervous!"

(**Message:** Once a year most congregations have an annual stewardship campaign. The truth is if you did it any more often, it would make a lot of church members very nervous! – See John 3:16a)

19. On Giving
An Internal Revenue Service agent called the pastor. He explained that a parishioner of his had reported that he had given $10,000 to the church. The tax man asked: "Did Mr. Ketterman give that amount?" The pastor paused; finally she spoke: "No, but he will! *He will!*"

  (**Application:** In Luke 6:38 our Lord declares that in giving we receive – eternal treasure! See also: II Samuel 24:18-25. Do we ever offer God a "white elephant" gift that "costs…nothing?")

*****

20. Difficulty of giving Thanks
A young woman entered a convent. The order she joined was a very strict one. Besides committing to poverty, chastity, and obedience, she had to also accept the discipline of silence. She would not speak for any reason for a year! Then at the end of her first year, she would be able to speak two words.

That year seemed as though it would never end! But finally the Mother Superior called her in to speak her two words. As she stood before her leader she said: "Food rotten!" The Mother Superior nodded in recognition that her complaint had been heard, and excused her.

A year later the sister returned. When asked for her two words she said, "Bed hard." Once again the Mother Superior nodded, then excused her.

The third year was especially long and hard for the novice, but she endured it. Finally the day came to stand before her Mother Superior. This time she exclaimed: "I quit!" To which the Mother Superior replied: "Well, good riddance! For ever since you got here, all you have done is complain!"

  (**Application:** It is difficult to be thankful in all circumstances. See: I Thessalonians 5:18)

*****

21. Let me have your Attention
An older Irish priest found it difficult to hold his congregation's attention during his sermons. Finally he went to the bishop for advice. The bishop

said: "Next Sunday, when it comes time for your message, tell your people: 'I am in love with a woman!' Then tell them that you have been in love with her for 35 years. You will have them on the edge of their seats! Then tell them that the woman is the blessed Mother, the Virgin Mary. They will be wide awake, and ready to listen!" The old priest thanked the bishop and left.

The next Sunday he began his sermon as the bishop had instructed by announcing: "I am in love with a beautiful woman! In fact I have been in love with her for 35 years." Well, the congregation was not only alert, but abuzz with whispers. Then he paused. A blank look came over his face. Finally he said: "For the life of me I cannot remember her name!"

(This story is good to use before beginning to speak. Otherwise its applications are limited)

*****

22. Sin has Consequences
Gary took his six year old out for a ride in his new convertible. He drove out on the freeway. Suddenly he had the urge to see how fast his new automobile would go! Turning to his son in the back seat, he said, "Son, if you see someone wearing a blue uniform and riding a motorcycle coming up behind us, be sure and tell Daddy!" Daddy was going to busy watching the road.

Off they went. Within a few seconds they were going 80 miles an hour. Suddenly he heard from the back seat: "Daddy, the man you were looking for has arrived!"

(**Message:** "Be sure your sins will find you out!" Numbers 32:23b)

*****

23. Challenges of the Job
The Reverend Edwin McNeill Poteat asked his facility manager to change the bulletin board on the church lawn. He explained that since he had not decided on the Sunday morning sermon, he wanted his manager to just put up the title of the evening message. Later he could post the morning title.

At noon the pastor left for lunch, and was horrified to read: "11:00 a.m.: 'The Minister will Preach' 7:00 p.m.: 'What the Fool Said.'"

(**Message:** Paul said: "I am speaking as a fool." II Corinthians 11:21b)

*****

24. Importance of Honesty

The pastor invited the parents of the one year old to be baptized, to come forward. Her four year old brother came too, with eyes wide open to take it all in. The pastor spoke concerning the purpose of infant baptism. Then, at the appropriate moment, she reached to take the child from her father. Suddenly the little brother piped up: "Be careful. She bites!"

(**Message:** The truth will also save your life… your soul!)

*****

25. Mysteries

A young girl asked her father: "Daddy, what holds up the world?" Not wanting to try and explain orbiting satellites and gravitational pull, he said simply: "The earth rests on the back of a giant elephant." "Daddy," came the reply, "What does the elephant stand on?" Realizing where this was going, he said simply: "Well, honey, it is elephants all the way down!"

(**Message:** There are some things which are too difficult for us to understand. One of those is God!)

*****

26. You can Know!

Dr. Wallace Chappell told in a sermon of a time when he was preaching a revival in a small town in Tennessee. Shortly before the evening service, he went for a stroll in the neighborhood around the church. As he passed a house, a dog started barking ferociously from a fenced in yard. Down the street, just out of sight, another joined in. Then over in the next block, yet another joined the chorus. "But," he said, "it was only the first dog that knew what he was barking about!"

(**Message:** Romans 8:16 reads: "It is the Spirit himself bearing witness with our spirit that we are children of God…" – We can "know in whom we have believed!" II Timothy 1:12)

*****

27. Marriage
A woman was asked if her husband believed in life after death. "Why," she said, "John? He doesn't even believe in life after supper!"
    (**Message:** It takes two committed persons to make a marriage! "Love" means giving! It is work!)

*****

28. Bridge to No Where?
Justice Oliver Wendell Holmes boarded a train. As the train started down the track, the conductor began his rounds of collecting the tickets. When he came to the famous jurist, he was shuffling through his briefcase. Finally, he had to admit that he could not find it. "That is all right Justice Holmes," said the conductor, "you can give it to me when you find it, or mail it to us later." "Oh, no, you don't understand," replied Holmes, "I need the ticket to know where I am going!"
    (**Message:** Jesus said, "I am the way, the truth, and the life…" John 14:6 – When we have Him we know where we are going!)

*****

29. Perfect Man?
A woman wrote "Dear Abby" saying: "I am a single woman who is 40 years old. I would like to meet a man of a similar age who has no bad habits." Abby replied: "So would I!"
    (**Message:** The trouble is: "All have sinned and fallen short of the glory of God!" Romans 3:23)

*****

30. On Fire for Christ?
A man from a non-liturgical church visited one that was very formal. After the service he shook the pastor's hand, and said: "You know I kind of like your lethargy!"
    (**Application:** "I know your works: you are neither cold nor hot.

Would that you were cold or hot! So, because you are lukewarm, and neither cold nor hot, I will spew you out of my mouth," says the Lord. Revelation 3:15-16)

*****

31. The Essence of life
An Oklahoma oilman died. His instructions were that he was to be buried in his Cadillac. The funeral director hustled around and arranged for a crane to be there on the day of the funeral. The grave had to be dug exceptionally large. Finally, all was in order. On the day of the funeral the deceased, according to his expressed wishes, was placed behind the wheel of the automobile. The crowd gathered. The pastor spoke a few words and offered up a prayer. That was the cue for the crane driver to lift the car and slowly lower it into the grave. As his old friend was passing from sight, Tom was heard to murmur: "Now, THAT'S living!"

(**Message:** No – no! That is DEATH! – How often our gadgets cause us to confuse the two!)

*****

32. Patience?
When I go to my grave they will not say, "He sure was a patient man!" While attending seminary at Emory University in Atlanta, we set out one Sunday afternoon to see the sights. We ended up in a small town south of Atlanta. I managed to get behind a driver going 15 miles per hour. After a few blocks I decided to pass the elderly gentleman. I went around, and up over a hill, and suddenly saw the barricade.

It was a dead end street! So, I pulled into a driveway to turn around, and sure enough, back up the hill the elderly gentleman, who had made the same mistake was turning around also. Now he was back in front once more!

(**Message:** "Wait … in patience!" Romans 8:25 – Lord: "Teach me the *patience* of unanswered prayer!" – Hymn: "Spirit of God Descend Upon My Heart" by George Croly – See also Galatians 5:22)

*****

33. We all blunder!
A novice starting out in the ministry was advised by an older pastor: "When you are speaking and your mind goes blank, simply quote scripture until you get your train of thought back, then go on."

Sure enough, during his second wedding he went blank. Panic struck first, then remembering the sage's advice, a scripture came to mind: "Father, forgive them for they know not what they do!"

(**Message:** "Therefore, if anyone thinks he/she stands take heed lest he/she fall!" I Corinthians 10:12)

*****

34. Repentance Possible?
Michael Soles of Auburn, California had just turned sixteen. Eager to get his driver's license, he went for the test. When his name was finally called, a meek little man greeted him cheerily. They went out and got into the car that was parked right in front of the license bureau. Both put on their seat belts. Then Mike pushed down on the clutch, put the car in gear, looked over his right shoulder to see if anyone was coming, revved the engine, popped the clutch, and crashed through the bureau's plate glass window! The examiner staggered out of the car in a state of shock, his clipboard still clutched in his hand. Mike, who was also shaken, asked: "Can I try that again?"

(**Message:** There are times in life when we wish we could go back and try that again!)

*****

35. Sin is All Around!
A young pastor arrived at his first church. Noting that it was situated beside a busy avenue, he decided to capitalize on the opportunity. So he put on the church sign: "If Tired of Sin – Come on in!" A few days later someone added: "If not, call 867-3393."

(**Message:** "Let us not grow weary in well-doing, for in due season we shall reap, if we do not lose heart." Galatians 6:9)

*****

36. Temptation
Back in the days of prohibition, a preacher was waxing long on the evils of alcohol. At the climax to his sermon he cried: "If I could, I would take all the liquor in this county and throw it into the river!" With that he sat down as the choir arose and sang: "Shall We Gather at the River!"

　　　(**Message:** Temptation via the internet, and many other sources is a reality Christians must do battle with daily!)

*****

37. Prayer – or -- Nation
A couple was with a tour in Washington D.C. As their tour guide was taking them through the Capitol building, she pointed to a gentleman, and said: "He is the congressional chaplain, someone asked, "Does he pray for the House or the Senate?" The guide smiled, and said: "He gets up, looks at the Congress, then prays for the *country!*"

　　　(**Application:** Human institutions all come out lacking. We need the Power that comes through prayer!)

*****

38. Christianity Lite
Back in the early 1970s we lived across the street from a woman who we learned, never attended worship. One day we invited her to church. She replied, "I am a Christian, but I am just not practicing it at the present."

　　　(**Message:** Being a Christian is more than giving mental assent to some beliefs. It involves ACTION! See: Matthew 7:21; 10:38; 16:24-25)

*****

39. The Presence of God – OR – Greatness
Back in the days of innocence, Oliver Wendell Holmes went for a walk one summer's evening. A little girl came out of her yard and walked with him. Suddenly, she heard her mother call her for supper. As she turned to run home, the famous jurist said: "Young lady, when you get home, and your mother asks you where you have been, tell her you have been walking with Oliver Wendell Holmes." Unimpressed, she replied: "And when you get home, tell your wife you have been walking with Mary Susanna Brown!"

(**Message:** Too often we fail to recognize the One who walks with us! See: Luke 24:13-31a)

*****

40. All of us have our Foibles!
A pastor returned to the first church he had served, to attend a funeral. As he visited with old friends, and caught up on the news, he asked one man: "Tell me about your Dad." "Oh, father died three years ago." "I am sorry to hear that," commented the pastor. After the funeral there were more persons to meet and greet. Then he came across the gentleman whose Dad had died. Weary of mind, he shook his hand again, and said: "Now tell me again about your Dad." The parishioner looked a little startled then said: "He is just as dead as he was a while ago!"

(**Message:** Be patient with others, for we all make mistakes! – See Romans 3:23)

*****

41. Witnessing
The pastor of a Riverside, California church decided he would visit each of the children's classes one summer. His first group was the 4 year olds. He entered the room, and the teacher asked: "Boys and girls do you know who this is?" Hesitantly one little girl answered: "God?" "No," said the teacher, "but he works for God." After the clergyman explained some of his duties, the same little girl interrupted: "Next time bring God with you. I've never seen Him!"

(**Message:** You and I re-present God as Christians! i.e. We must "present" Him again and again to the world. For we are a "letters from Christ," Paul said in II Corinthians 3:3b)

*****

42. God's Providential Care
Father Anthony de Mello, S.J. tells of a priest who was working on his homily for Sunday on the providence of God. Suddenly he heard what sounded like an explosion! Watching from his study window he saw water beginning to rise in the street. People were running frantically for higher ground. Then it dawned upon him that the dam above the town must have burst!

At first he panicked too. Then he sat back down at his desk saying to himself, "I am preparing a message on God's protection. God must be testing me to see if I am going to believe what I am about to preach."

He went back to his sermon, even though he could hear the water gurgling under the front door downstairs. When he looked out, the water was everywhere! He raised his window to see the extent of the flood, when a rescue boat came by. "Hop in, Father," called the driver. But the priest assured him that he, a man of God, would be just fine!

Now the water was spilling into his room through the open window, so he thought it best to climb out onto the roof. He crawled out, and then up to the peak. Another boat pulled up, and above the idling motor someone called for the clergyman to get on board, because the dam had burst. But the priest said: "I have trusted in God all these years; I have no reason not to trust Him now!"

The water rose to his knees. It was now hard to keep his balance in the current! So, he climbed upon the chimney. As the water rose even more, yet another boat came. Its occupants also tried to get the priest to come to safety before it was too late. But again he insisted that God would protect him!

The water continued to rise. The priest drowned.

When he got to heaven, he was angry! He said to God: "There I was trusting in you. Why did you do nothing to save me?" God said: "Are you kidding? Why I sent three boats for you!"
     (**Message:** God expects us to participate in His miracles – in His providential care. Remember when the people of Israel were faced with the sea? God told Moses: "Why do you cry to me? Tell the people to go forward!" Exodus 14:15 – As they moved forward, only then, did He part the waters!)

*****

43. Marriage & Family
A couple was living in a two room townhouse with their five year old daughter. They decided to look for a larger place, since another baby was on the way. As they looked through a much larger three bedroom home, the little girl piped up to exclaim: "Look! Mommy, you won't have to sleep with Daddy anymore – you can have a room of your *own*!"

(**Message:** "… Now I know in part, then I shall understand fully…" I Corinthians 13:12b)

*****

44. Marriage
A Houston rabbi received a thank you for marrying a couple. The new bride wrote: "Dear Rabbi, I want to thank you for the beautiful way you brought my happiness to a conclusion!" (She *meant* to say "to *completion*.")

(**Message:** The bride was partially right! Marriage is not all happiness. Any two persons who live in such close proximity to each other, and share life so intimately, will "bump" into each other from time-to-time. Marriage is not something that happens one day in June, but it entails a lifetime of effort. Love demands that we work at it!)

*****

45. Marriage
She flew across the country to finally meet her three year old grandson. He was playing in the floor of his bedroom when the grandmother arrived. Her daughter ushered her in to see him. "Oh," she gushed, "you don't know me, but I am your grandmother on your mother's side."

Hardly looking up, the youngster responded: "I'll tell you right now, you're on the *wrong* side!" By Bennett Cerf in "Good for a Laugh"

(**Message:** "(Out of the) mouth of babes and infants thou hast founded a bulwark…" Psalm 8:2a How often our children gently remind us of our foibles.)

*****

46. Discipline of Children
It was Thanksgiving time for the small community. Down at the United Methodist Church the Sunday School teacher stood before her first and

second grade class. Before the class began, she had written all the children's names on the whiteboard. Now she asked the class to think of something they were thankful for, and she would write it by the corresponding student's name. One little boy thought hard. (He had had a rough morning!) Finally, he decided upon listing his mother. But before the teacher could get her marker, he called out: "No, change that – to my dog!"

(**Message:** Parenting is at best a challenge! Discipline is essential, but troubling to both to the parent and the child.)

*****

47. Parenting or Priorities
While flying from Chicago to Kansas City, a passenger overheard a concerned mother saying to her six year old, "Remember, honey, you must run to Dad and hug him, and *then* the dog!

(**Message:** Children, like us adults, sometimes fail the love test. What do we put before *them*?)

*****

48. Anger / Violence
Back in the horse and buggy days a Quaker was driving his buggy to town. Suddenly he was run off the road by another man. The Quaker was furious! He shook his fist in the air as he shouted: "I am not a violent man, but I hope that when thou gettest home thy mother crawls out from under thy front porch and bites thee!"

(**Message:** Righteous anger has its place! Ephesians 4:26)

*****

49. Humility?
The captain of the battleship saw the lights of an approaching ship. He had the signalman flash a warning: "Change your course 10 degrees to the south." Immediately came a reply: "Change *your* direction 20 degrees north." Infuriated the captain sent back: "This is a battleship! Change *your* course!" Again came a reply: "Change your course. This is a *lighthouse*!"

(**Message:** An humble disposition can save your life (soul)! James 4:6b)

50. Fear Justified?

I shall never forget our first Halloween at Broadway United Methodist Church in Springfield, Missouri. It was back in 1972. Hardly had we arrived at the parsonage in the downtown area, when we began to discover the crime in the area. Thieves broke into the church. A neighborhood house was obviously selling drugs. And the list goes on.

So, when Halloween rolled around we did not know what to expect! It was a typical Halloween with children accompanied by parents coming to our door. At 9:00 p.m. we turned off the porch light.

About 15 minutes later came a knock at the door. I answered to see what appeared to be two men adorned in costumes with masks. They said nothing. So, I started to close the door, when the first of the two tried to come on in. I put both hands on "his" shoulders and pushed him into the second, knocking them both off balance. As I was about to slam the door, the one I had pushed raised his hand to his mouth, and it was a *woman's* hand! Only then was it revealed that the pranksters were two middle-aged women in the church! And I had practically shoved them off the porch! (They lived in the suburbs where there was little crime, and failed to realize what my response might be!) They did not do any more trick-or-treating at the parsonage!

(**Application:** We often fear things which in reality are harmless. But even when our foes are real God is greater still! Note all the times in Scripture when God says: "Fear not!" Genesis 15:1; 26:24; 50:19-21 etc.)

*****

51. Marriage Trials

A man was planning to shingle the roof of his home. The roofer's price was more than he wanted to pay, so he thought: "I can do a job like that! After all it is a simple matter of getting the shingles in a row along the eave, then nailing them in place." He decided to start in the back of the house, since the afternoon sun would be striking there later on. To get prepared he threw a large rope up and over the peak of the roof. Then he tied it to the bumper of his car that he had parked in the driveway. He returned to the backyard, and climbed the extension ladder to the roof. Once there he tied the other end of the rope around his waist – just to be safe. Then he started nailing away.

All went well until his wife came hurrying out of the house. She did not see the rope. Jumped in the car, and backed out of the driveway! Only then did she hear her husband as he crested the gable of the roof flying through the air! She slammed on the brakes, but the damage was done. He crashed into the shrubs below. Well he survived, and amazingly their marriage did too!

(**Message:** Every marriage has its trials!)

*****

52. Uncertainties

Back in the early 1960s in Bagdad an American salesman, bound for an out-of-the-way desert village, boarded a small twin engine propeller plane. Hardly had he taken his seat when the pilot came back and said the plane had some serious engine troubles. The passengers got off, since the repairs were going to take a few hours. But an hour later they were asked to board again. "Do we have a different plane?" asked the salesman. "No," said the stewardess, "we have a different pilot!"

(**Message:** Life is filled with uncertainties!) (See: Psalm 23:4)

*****

53. "Be sure your sins will find you out!"
Numbers 32:23

A young preacher at First Baptist Church in Blairsville, Georgia was preaching at the Sunday evening service. As always, hardly had he begun when old John dozed off, sound asleep. But on this particular night a thunderstorm came rolling in. The lightning flashed and the thunder rattled the windows. Suddenly the power went out! Unable to see his notes, the quick thinking pastor asked everyone to spend some time in silent prayer.

The silence jolted John awake! He looked around, and could see no one! So he scrambled out of his aisle seat muttering for all to hear: "My God, they have gone off and left me!" Everyone burst into laughter!

When the lights did come back on a few minutes later, John was nowhere to be seen!

(**Message:** We do not always get caught in our sin daily, but in time we will!)

54. Teacher of Children

A Sunday School teacher was having problems with her fourth grade class. Several of the students had never been in church, and therefore knew nothing about the faith. Timmy was one such boy. On this Sunday they were trying to study the Lord's Prayer. But the students were just not listening! Finally, in desperation, she singled out the ring leader, Timmy. "Timmy! Will you repeat the Lord's Prayer for the class?" she asked. To her amazement Timmy began: "Our Father who art in heaven, *how did you know my name?*… Lead us not into *Penn Station,* but deliver us from evil…" The teacher did not have the nerve to correct him in front of the class! It was all she could do to keep a straight face!

(**Message:** Persons absorb more than we realize – even mischievous boys!)

*****

55. Fox hole Religion

Tom and Jim were two salesmen who were hoping to sell some implements to a farmer. His wife told them where they could find her husband on the backside of the field west of the house. So, they set out on foot. They got about halfway across this huge field when they saw a bull rushing toward them! The two men ran for dear life to a nearby tree. Somehow they both managed to get up the tree, just out of reach of the bull's horns. But their bovine attacker was in such a rage that he began to butt the tree. The tree began to sway, and the men were not sure how long they could hold on!

Knowing that his partner had been "religious" at one point in his childhood, Tom cried out: "Pray for us, Jim!" By now the tree's roots were loosening as it leaned back-and-forth! Finally Jim remembered a prayer his Dad used for before meals. So he cried out in a loud voice: "Lord! Make us truly grateful for what we are about to receive."

(**Application:** We do our best praying in the hour of our desperation!)

*****

56. Worry

Someone has said: "Do not let anyone tell you that worry does not help

– it does, for most of the things I worried about last year never happened!"

  (**Message:** Some of the early pioneers would worry about a stream they knew they were going to have to cross, for fear that it would be at flood stage, or in some other way might threaten them or their belongings. Thus, Abraham Lincoln was recorded as saying: "Never cross a stream until you get to it." – Our Lord said it this way: "Do not be anxious about tomorrow…" Matthew 6:34a)

*****

57. Security
The late Paul Harvey told of a man who was living in a rough section of Chicago. There were lots of break-ins in the area. As a result he was having trouble sleeping at night. Finally, he decided to purchase a pit bull. The owner said it was trained as a guard dog, so he figured that the peace of mind it would bring would make it worth the asking price of $1,000. He bought the dog, and took it home. That night he slept soundly! He got up the next morning all refreshed, but soon discovered that in the night someone had broken in, and stolen his dog!

  (**Message:** We are constantly looking for security, but true security is found in God alone! Jesus said: "Peace I leave with you, my peace I give unto you! John 14:27)

*****

58. Certainties
An elderly woman complained that her financial advisor wanted her to buy some long term bonds. She said: "At my age I'm not interested in anything long term! Why I don't even buy green bananas!"

  (**Message:** With her sense of humor, she will be laughing all the way to the Pearly Gates!)

*****

59. Honesty
Back in the days before air conditioning a family invited the pastor home for Sunday dinner. It was a very hot August day. The "woman of the house" had toiled over the hot wood cook stove frying a chicken, and

putting together a wonderful meal. Finally, all was ready. As they were seated around the table, she proudly asked her four year old to offer the prayer. In the presence of the preacher, the lad hesitated, so his mother said to him: "Honey, just say something you have heard me say." Agreeing, the lad bowed his head and prayed: "Lord, why did we invite this preacher here on a hot day like this!"

(**Message:** Leave it to a child to tell it like it is!)

*****

60. Humbling Experience – or – Understanding

A young pastor in Iowa was hosting his District Superintendent one Sunday. The Superintendent's name was Dr. Crow. The young preacher was very nervous having his supervisor in the congregation. He welcomed him and introduced him to the congregation.

All went well until the Pastoral Prayer. On the spur of the moment the pastor decided to call on his guest to stand and offer the prayer. But it did not come out the way he intended! He said, "Dr. Pray, would you *crow* for us?"

(**Message:** We can understand others faux pas, because we have had our share of them!)

*****

61. Nervous blunders

The Reverend Rex Knowles tells of a pastor's nightmare that occurred at a wedding where he was officiating. He was just starting his ministry when he had his first wedding. His nerves got the best of him when he switched the names of the best man and his brother, the groom. So, at a critical moment he asked: "Robert will you take this woman to be your wife?" Shaken, the best man answered: "Well, I asked her, but she said she preferred my brother!"

(**Message:** We can make some big blunders when we let our nerves get the best of us.)

*****

62. Life's Humbling Experiences

Maldwyn Edwards went back to a church he had served, on the occasion of its centennial celebration. Soon after he arrived, a dear lady drew him aside to bring him up to date on her life's history, since the days when Dr. Edwards was pastor there. Finally, she said: "Of course you heard about my dear Albert? He has gone to be with the Lord." Edwards responded: "Oh, I am sorry to hear that." But that did not sound right for a pastor to be sorry that someone went to Heaven, so he added: "What I meant to say was I am *glad* to hear that!" Still that seemed inappropriate, so he gave a final stab at it: "What I *really* meant was I am surprised!"

(**Message:** When you find yourself in a hole – quit digging!)

*****

63. Buzzards or Bees? / Gossiping

We divide the population of the world in different ways. We can distinguish a people by their race, country of origin, socio-economic standing, religious affiliation, or any of a number of other ways. But consider that we can be divided into "buzzards" and "bees."

Buzzards can be seen soaring high in the heavens looking for a carcass to devour. They feed on the tragedies and failures of others in the animal kingdom. When they see such remains, they swoop down and enjoy a good feast.

Bees, on the other hand, search out the sweet nectar of the beautiful flowers. They are focused upon such, for their energy, their very lives would soon be sapped away if they were to focus on something else.

Which are you: a buzzard or a bee? Do you focus on the disasters, moral failings, or physical ailments of others? Or, like the bee, do you focus on what is good in others; what is beautiful, and sweet? What is your focus?

(**Message:** The focus of our lives determines the persons we will become, and the one we will be remembered by. – See James 1:26 also I Peter 3:10.)

*****

64. Falling Short

In the hills of eastern Kentucky, back in the days when school principals could use corporal punishment to keep unruly students in line, ten year old Tom was sent to the office. He had been there several times before, so the principal was weary of Tom's behavior. He grabbed him up by the shoulders to eye level, and said, "Tom! I think the devil has a hold of you!" With trembling voice, Tom responded, "I think so, too, sir."

    (**Message:** We fall short of the Christ like life! – "Wretched person that I am, who will deliver me from this body of death? Thanks be to God through our Lord Jesus Christ!" Romans 7:24-25a)

*****

65. Interruptions

The Reverend Jaraslav Vajda tells how he was troubled that his organist slipped out of the service as soon as the sermon began. One Sunday he began his sermon with a story from the Civil War. Sure enough the organist began his exit from the sanctuary, out the side door that opened to a stairwell. Jaraslav told of a soldier who at the height of battle, thought he heard the command to "Charge!" Leaping out of the trench he started across no-man's land. Seeing him, the Commander yelled: "Come back here you fool!" Suddenly the sermon was interrupted with someone crashing up the stairs that led to the sanctuary. Soon the organist appeared from the side door to take his place, and never left it again!

    (**Message:** Oftentimes in life the *unintended* changes our course – for the better!)

*****

66. Mirrored Failures

My wife, Ginya, had a "special" birthday a few years back. Concerned that she had been showing some signs of having difficulty hearing, I found her seated with her back to me. I was about 10 feet away, so I decided to put her to the test. I said in a normal voice. "Ginya, can you hear me?" No response. I moved to about 8 feet behind her. "Ginny, can you hear me?" No response. Thinking now I was onto a real problem, I moved to 6 feet and said, "Ginny, can you hear me?" She said, "For the *third* time, YES!"

    (**Application:** Often the weaknesses we see in others are our own!)

67. Only in Court
A judge who had served down in the Ozarks for a number of years tells of one defendant who was on the stand. The prosecutor was asking him a series of leading questions. He said, "Sir, is it not true that you were shot in the fracas?" "Oh, no sir!" he replied, "I was shot somewhere between my fracas and my navel."

(**Application:** This one is best left without application!)

*****

68. Honesty Pays
Back in the days before refrigeration, a butcher had a barrel behind the counter that he put the chickens in that he was preparing to sell. He put some water in the barrel, then a lot of ice on top. Then he would place the chickens he had cleaned down in the cold slush.

Late one day a woman came in wanting a hen to bake. Having only one chicken left, the butcher reached down into the icy depths and pulled out the remaining chicken. "How's that," he asked. "Don't you have a larger one?" she responded. Fearful of losing the sale, he took the bird and plunged it deep into the barrel stirred it around, and then pulled it back out again. "How about this one?" he offered. "Fine," she said, "I'll take them *both!*"

(Message: Even little lies can come back to haunt us!)

*****

69. Consequences
A pastor visited an elderly widow late one afternoon. The widow asked her pastor if she would like a cup of coffee. She agreed, so while she was in the kitchen brewing some coffee, the pastor spied a bowl of peanuts. She ate one, then another. By the time the hostess got back with the refreshment, she had eaten almost half the bowl. Embarrassed with herself, she said, "Mrs. Smith, I am so sorry! I sat here and ate most of your peanuts." "Think nothing of it, honey," said the widow patting her on the knee. "With these dentures, all I can do is suck the chocolate off of them!" (After telling this one Sunday, a layman – Richard Splitter – left a bag of chocolate covered peanuts on the pulpit for me to find.)

(**Message:** Sin also comes with surprises / consequences! – See: Romans 6:23)

70. Discipline
A young lad was practicing his piano lesson. A salesman came to the door, and heard him. When the boy answered the door, the salesman asked: "Is your mother home?" "What do *you* think?" came the reply.

  (**Message:** Discipline is difficult on any level! – See: Romans 7:15)

*****

71. Fear
It was a dark night when a thunderstorm came rolling in. The lightning flashed. The thunder rolled. One bolt hit nearby, lighting up the sky! The thunder that quickly followed shook the house! Six year old Tracy called out: "Mother, I'm scared!" Her mother went in to check on her. "Honey," she said reassuringly, you need not be afraid; the Lord is with you!" "I know, Mom," said the frightened girl, "but I want someone in here with skin on them!"

  (**Message:** He who calmed the winds and the sea cries out to us: "Fear not!" – Read Matthew 8:26)

*****

72. Discipline
Years ago in a church down in Kentucky a child was trying his parents' patience during the worship service. A finger to the lip signaling to be quiet was usually enough, but not this day! The rowdiness grew. Finally, his father whisked him up under his arm, and headed for the door. As they were passing to the outside, the lad was heard to say, "You all pray for me, you hear!"

  (**Message:** Hebrews 12:6a declares: "The Lord disciplines him who he loves.")

*****

73. Frustrations
It was Christmas time, and a father was pushing his son in the grocery cart through the aisles, doing their shopping. With the list in hand, he was filling the basket. His young son was not helping. In one aisle he tossed a can of pumpkin out of the cart. His father was heard to say, "Calm down, Albert!" In the next aisle the lad snatched a box of cereal off the shelf.

Again, his father said, "Everything will be all right. Calm down now, Albert." A woman who had observed all this for several aisles finally stopped the man. "Sir," she said, "I realize that it is none of my business, but why do you tolerate such behavior from Albert?" "But, you don't understand, lady," said the father, "I am Albert!"

(**Application:** Life is filled with frustrations. Some of which you *can* do something about!)

*****

74. Conflict Resolved!
In Chicago the Methodists and the Baptists were at odds with each other. The two denominations had churches in the same block. Apparently, the Methodists had a very small parking lot for their needs, so they would park in the Baptist lot. The Baptists did not want to cause trouble, but the fact remained that they often needed the parking spaces. One Sunday a Baptist deacon came up with a "diplomatic cure." He and some of the other deacons put bumper stickers on all the cars in their lot which read: "I am Proud to Be a Baptist!" – It was a sticky problem for the Methodists, but they took the hint!

(**Message:** Love can triumph over all differences! See I Corinthians 13.)

*****

75. Compliments
The Lay Leader of the church congratulated the pastor on being appointed to serve the congregation for another year. Then, trying to be complimentary he added, "Why, we didn't know what sin was – until you came!"

(**Message:** We can be grateful for those who teach us what sin is, and Christ's cure!)

*****

76. Witnessing - or - Baptism
A mother discovered her six year old dunking his little brother in a mud hole in the backyard. Horrified, she ran out and stopped him. "Young man," she said angrily, "What do you think you are doing to your little

brother?" "We are playing church," he explained. "Church?" she asked. "Yes, I was baptizing him in the 'name of the Father, and of the Son, and in the hole-he-goes.'"

(**Message:** We must be careful in regard to *what* message our children get from us.)

*****

77. Procrastination or Holy Habits
Way down in the Ozarks a country preacher was waxing long on his message when he used the word "procrastination." After the service one of his parishioners asked him what the meaning of the word was. Not sure of the meaning himself, he hesitated, then answered: "Why that is one of the doctrines of the Methodist Church!"

(**Message:** It is easy for us to practice procrastination when it comes to the holy habits of prayer, worship, study of the Word, and service in love.)

*****

78. Indecision
Back in the early 1920s my grandfather was driving the family across town in Joplin, Missouri. He was driving a new touring car with the top down. Grandfather was very inexperienced at driving, so when he came to the streetcar track, and saw the train coming, first he hesitated. Then at the last minute he thought he could beat the streetcar. So, he gunned the car forward onto the tracks. Seeing that a crash was imminent, he slammed on the brakes, and tried to back up! Well, he was hit broadside, sliding the automobile around into the side of the streetcar! My father was holding a dozen eggs in a brown paper bag, and when the collision occurred, he instinctively clutched the eggs – smashing them all over his stomach and chest! A passenger in the streetcar looked down upon the wreckage, and screamed, for she was sure that Dad had burst open!

(**Message:** Indecision can be costly sometimes!)

*****

79. Baptism
The young couple came forward to have their infant twins baptized. At a particularly solemn moment the pastor asked: "What names are to be

given to these children?" The nervous father answered: "Steak and Kidney." "No!" gasped his wife, "It is Kate and Sydney!"

(**Message:** We have all made our share of mistakes at critical moments!)

*****

80. Unbelievable

Back in the days of innocence, a man was driving his Cadillac down a country road when he came upon a boy walking with his dog in the same direction. He stopped, and asked the lad if he wanted a ride. The boy said, "Sure!" and climbed in, and continued to hold the door open so his dog could get in too. "Oh, no!" exclaimed the driver, "I can't have your dog in my car. He can run beside us. I won't go very fast." The boy agreed. The driver drove along slowly – about 20 miles per hour. After a while he asked: "Is your dog keeping up?" "Sure! No problem." The driver speeded up to 30 miles per hour. "How's he doing?" The lad looked out, and said: "He is right here!" The driver decided to speed on up to 45. "Left him behind yet?" asked the driver. "No, he is panting, but he is right beside me!" With that the driver slammed on his brakes. The car skidded to a halt. In disbelief the man got out, and walked around the car. There was the dog! "What's that hanging out of his mouth?" asked the driver. The boy said, "Oh that's his *tail*. He's not used to stopping that *quick!*"

(**Message:** Some things are unbelievable! See Luke 24:11)

*****

81. Blunders

In 1985, while I was serving as District Superintendent of the Kansas City North District of the United Methodist Church, Bishop W.T. Handy told us that when he first came on the Missouri Area, he visited all the churches his first year. It was quite an undertaking! The superintendents knew his schedule, and were to have the pastor present on the day of his visit. In one small town in mid-Missouri, the D.S. drove the bishop by the parsonage to get the pastor to go with them to the church. The pastor was in the yard, mowing grass. The D.S. called to him. He stopped the mower, and then admitted that he had forgotten that the bishop was coming. Then added: "I need to finish up here, but you all can go on over to the church. It is locked, but the window to the left of the door is always unlocked. You can crawl in through there." Needless to say, the bishop did not crawl through the window to see the church. – What happened to the pastor? Well, you might say he was not a rising star!

(**Application:** Paul said it is important to "pay honor to whom honor is due." Romans 13:7c)

*****

82. Confession of Sin
A protestant man went to a priest one Saturday afternoon, because he had heard that if he confessed to a priest he could be forgiven. His Catholic friend had coached him about where to go and what to do.

"Father, I have sinned," he said. "Yes, my son, go on," replied the priest. "Well, I stole some plywood from the lumberyard, and built a dog house." "That indeed is a wrong," declared the priest, "But you cannot take the lumber back, so if you will offer a few 'Our Father' prayers, and trust God's mercy, God will forgive you."

There was a pause. "I also built a shed for a shop in my backyard," confessed the man. "Well, this is more serious," responded the priest. "If you will do some deeds of mercy for five persons you meet this week, then God will forgive you."

"I don't know how to say it, but I also built a room on the back of my house," confided the man. "Now this IS very serious," said the priest. Now he had to reflect for a moment. Finally, he said, "Sir, do you know how to make a novena?" (A novena is nine days of prayer.) "No, father, I do not, but if you've got the plans, I've got the plywood!"

(**Application:** When we *truly* turn from our sins – that involves repaying our debt if possible – God *will* in fact forgive us! See Acts 26:20b; & I John 1:5-10)

*****

83. Marriage
Momma shouted to Papa, who was hard of hearing, "Judd, we've been married 60 years now. I want you to know that you are *'tried-and-true!'*"

Judd said: "What?" So, she repeated: "I said, '*You – are – tried and true!*'" "Well," said Judd, "I'm tired of you too!"

(**Application:** We all have our moments! Yet, a beautiful marriage has at its heart an abiding commitment! – Read again I Corinthians 13:8a)

*****

84. Witness

A preacher was building a trellis in his backyard. As he was hammering away he sensed someone was standing, watching him. Looking up he saw a neighbor boy staring at him. "Jimmy, did you want something?" he asked. "No," he replied, "I was just wondering what a preacher said when he hit his thumb."

(**Message:** Whether we realize it or not there are always young eyes watching us!)

*****

85. Husbands

A man came into the doctor's office with both ears bandaged. The nurse asked him what happened. "I was ironing to appease my wife, while watching football on television," he explained. "The phone rang at a critical point, and I put the iron up to my ear!" "Yes," responded the nurse, trying to be sympathetic, "but what happened to the other ear?" "The guy called back!"

(**Message:** Give me your undivided attention!)

*****

86. Swearing

President Harry Truman was known to use swear words with some regularity! One time he was speaking to a group of agriculturalists, and he used the word "manure." (That seems awfully innocent today!) Later one of those at the convention complained to Bess Truman that the president should not use such gross terms. Her reply: "You don't know how long it took me to get him to say, 'manure'!"

(**Message:** There are a lot of things worse than crude speech!)

87. On Doing Good

Annual Conference for United Methodist clergy and laity is a time when some heated debates take place. One such conference was particularly heated. Afterward a pastor told me: "Preachers are like manure; piled all together they produce a lot of heat, but spread over the countryside, they produce a lot of good!"

(**Application:** Pray "thy kingdom come, thy will be done…" See Matthew 6:9ff)

*****

88. Indecision

A Baptist Church in Wisconsin extended calls to the Reverend John Melvin to be their assistant pastor, and the Reverend Philip Johnson to be their senior pastor. John quickly accepted the position of assistant to the senior pastor, but Phil wanted to think about it. The assistant pastor moved his family into the parsonage for him, but still no word from Phil. Finally, the head of the search committee sent Phil an email that read simply: "Matthew 11:3." An appropriate verse which reads: "Are you he who is to come, or shall we look for another?"

(**Message:** Decisions can be hard to make! But after prayer and reflection there comes a time to ACT!)

*****

89. Too Busy

Father kept bringing home work from his company, to do in the evenings. His daughter, who was in the first grade, asked him why. He explained that there was so much work to do he could not do it in an eight hour day. With that her face lit up! She knew the solution! "Daddy, why don't they put you in a slower group?"

(**Message:** Sometimes we need to be put in a "slower group" – to "be still" and come to know God! Psalm 46:10)

*****

90. Determination

It was a very rainy season. In fact it rained so much that a family was flooded out of their home. With the waters rising rapidly they had to leave the downstairs. Once upstairs, they thought it best to climb out onto the roof and wait for help to arrive. As the mother and her two children waited, they noticed a hat go floating by. Then the hat turned, and came back by. Junior said, "Momma, what is that?" "Oh," she said, "That's your Dad. He said he was going to mow the lawn come hell or high water!"

(**Application:** Determination is required for many tasks to succeed. In Ruth 1:18 it says that Ruth "was determined" to go with her mother-in-law while facing great odds against her!)

*****

91. Prayer

A grandmother in our congregation told me how afraid of storms her grandson was. One evening he was staying at her house when a thunderstorm came rolling in. The lightning flashed. The thunder shook the house! With trembling voice he said, "Grandma, are you afraid?" "Well yes," she admitted, "storms make me nervous too. But I just pray: 'Lord, watch over me in Jesus' name. The Lord has always taken care of me." Unimpressed he went back to watching television. Suddenly, a *huge* bolt of lightning struck nearby! Before the thunder could roll, he turned and said, "Grandmother, how'd that prayer go?"

(**Message:** It pays to be "prayed up" in the good times, so that when the storms come we will be ready.)

*****

92. Measuring Up

I became good friends with Jab White while serving the United Methodist Church in Warsaw, Missouri. Jab was the editor of the local newspaper, and had a delightful sense of humor! He told the following story under his column: "Jab's Gab."

A local patrolman was working a sobriety checkpoint when he pulled a car over. He walked up to the driver's door, and could not believe his eyes! In the passenger seat beside him was a rack of knives!

The driver said, "I know this looks suspicious to have all these knives beside me, but I am a juggler and have just performed at a youngster's birthday party. Tell you what, let me show you what I do." The patrolman agreed, for after all if he was at all inebriated he would not be able to juggle the knives. So, the man got out, and began to perform his stunt. Soon he had six knives whirling in the air.

Just then, the lawman felt a tap on his shoulder. Turning around he saw a gentleman who had just been stopped by the checkpoint. "Officer," he said nervously, "You might as well go ahead and arrest me, because there is absolutely no way I can pass *this* test!"

    (**Message:** When we stand beside Jesus, our merits seem as nothing! Only grace can save us, and we have that in our Lord! See Romans 5:16)

*****

93. Marriage
A woman was feeling quite despondent about her marriage. Her husband was unaware of the source of the problem, but agreed to go with her to a psychologist to see if she could get some help. After just two sessions the doctor announced: "The treatment I prescribe is quite simple." With that he got up, went across the room, and gave the woman a kiss on the cheek. Then he stepped back to reveal a smile on her face. "See," he announced, "That is all she needs to get to feel good again." To which the husband replied: "Great, doc, I'll bring her in every Tuesday!"

    (**Message:** Sometimes couples miss the obvious in their relationship. The answer is often quite simple.)

*****

94. Judgment
A farmer was losing apples from his orchard to a thief. The guilty party had been caught several times, warned, but still he persisted. Finally, in desperation the farmer came up with a plan. It would surely stop the thief once-and-for-all!

He took a shell to his old 10 gauge shotgun, emptied out the lead shot, and put it in the chamber of the gun. When it was about time for the thief to make his appearance, he cooked up some oatmeal. Then he took a cup of oatmeal, and his gun to the orchard. Beside the entrance to the trees, he rigged a trip-line, then anchored the gun to a tree. Finally, he tied the trip line to the trigger. Now it was time to pour the oatmeal down the barrel.

A couple of hours later, about dusk, the thief crept toward the orchard. But he did not go far when he set off the shotgun! A hot blast of oatmeal struck him in the side of the head! Terrified, he raced from the orchard, and down the road. He could feel the warm mixture oozing down his neck. He ran until he came upon a man on the road. Grabbing him by both shoulders, he cried: "How long can a person live with his brains blown out?"

    (**Message:** God is not only a God of love, but of judgment! The scripture says: "The Lord disciplines the one he loves!" Hebrews 12:6 We either live *with* the grain of the universe, or against it! If we go against it – we get a lot of "splinters.")

*****

95. Answers

She sat before the children for their sermon. "What is it that collects nuts for winter, climbs trees, and has a bushy tail?" she asked.

An eager boy waved his hand. She responded: "Yes, Jimmy what is it?" Jimmy thought for a moment, then replied: "Well, I know the answer is supposed to be Jesus, but it sure sounds like a squirrel!"

    (**Application:** In life we often *want* answers, but what we need is Jesus!)

*****

96. Death

One young pastor conducted a funeral. She was trying to make the point that our soul leaves the body at death. The soul is gone, but the body remains behind. Suddenly an analogy came to mind. Thus she declared in dramatic form as she gestured toward the casket: "What we have here is just the shell! Just the shell!! The *nut* is gone!" (She *wanted* to be gone too!)

    (**Message:** We prefer to deny death – like a lad whistling through the cemetery – yet, it is for real!)

97. Pedigree
Mark Twain wrote that he once spent $25 to have his family history researched. Then $50 to try to cover it up again!

    (**Message:** None can rest on their laurels of pedigree! We must rest alone in Him who is our Father!)

*****

98. Embarrassments
A colleague in the ministry, Dan, shared with a group of us his most embarrassing moment. It was a beautiful July morning – a good day to go fishing. Dan did not have anything on the schedule that afternoon that could not wait, so he decided he would go. First he wanted to get a new lure that had been landing the bass. Then he had the monthly Ministerial Alliance luncheon to go to. He had promised to take his friend, the pastor of the Christian Church with him.

At 11 a.m. Dan went by the hardware store and purchased the lure. It was one of those long, hot dog shaped jobs with a treble hook on both ends. He got the lure, went out and jumped in his two-seater sporty convertible. He threw the lure over in the passenger seat. Since it was such a nice day, he decided to put put the top down. Then he drove by to get his friend.

The Christian Church pastor came running out, jumped in, and landed on the lure! Dan now had his first catch of the day! For the lure embedded in the sitting-down-part of the preacher! In pain he tried to rise up, but the other end of the lure was embedded in the leather seat. – Now both seats were hooked!

Dan got down in the floorboard so he might see under his anguished – (former) friend. He was able to unhook the end that was embedded in his car seat – his biggest concern – but the end that was hooked to the preacher was not as easy! Every time he wiggled the lure his friend writhed in pain. So, Dan gave up, started the car, and raced toward the town's only clinic.

Now picture this! His friend had to make the drive resting on his shoulders and heels, for he could not sit down, for fear of driving the barbs deeper! Soon they arrived with a screech at the doctor's office. Dan ran around, opened the car door, and literally had to lift his companion up off his shoulders into an upright position. Then the two of them made their way into the office – the injured one with a lure wagging behind him.

In this small town, everyone in the waiting room knew them both – adding insult to injury! Dan felt responsible to tell the receptionist that his fellow pastor needed immediate attention due to the fishing lure embedded in his backside! She held back a laugh as she disappeared to tell the doctor.

Laughter had already spread through the waiting room by the time the nurse invited them back to the examination room. The doctor, who was a member of Dan's church, said: "Dan, you have been taking scripture too literally – about being a 'fisher of men!'"
(**Message:** Witnessing to others needs to have the "barbs" removed!)

*****

99. Pledges
Well before sunrise two men made a long trek into the national forest to go turkey hunting. They moved along quietly, listening for the turkeys as they fly from perches high in the trees. But they heard none.

About mid-morning, having gone several miles with no luck, they realized they were lost! They followed their instincts, but soon were back where they started!

Finally, one said to the other: "Cheer up, Sam, it is Pledge Sunday tomorrow at my church. If we are still lost, I know the Finance Committee will find me!"
(**Message:** For a variety of good reasons Pledge Sunday is important in every church.)

*****

100. Embarrassments / Humility
A rather religious family bought a parrot. They soon discovered that the parrot could be an embarrassment, for it had been owned by a man who

swore a lot, and the bird picked up some choice words. They had been told that the parrot would not talk when its cage was covered, so on Sundays they covered his cage.

Late one Wednesday afternoon the family was surprised with a visit from the pastor. As the mother was welcoming him in, her son raced to cover the parrot's cage! They were about to be seated in the living room, when from over in the corner came: "Damn short week!"
     (**Message:** Life has a way of humbling us – of knocking us off our pedestals in the most inopportune moments! See James 4:6b)

*****

101. Grace
A young lad accidentally broke his mother's favorite vase. She was in the kitchen fixing supper, and did not hear the commotion. He crept out of the den, and into the kitchen. His mother saw him slipping by, so she asked: "What's the matter, honey?" He said, "I'm going to my room to talk to God." "Is there anything that we need to talk about?" she asked. "No, because you will scold me, and God will forgive me and forget all about it!" – See Jeremiah 31:34c
     (**Message:** Ephesians 2:8 declares: "For by grace you have been saved through faith, and this is not of your own doing, it is the gift of God.")

*****

102. Repent
A house painter agreed to paint the Baptist Church in town. He bid the job at a fair price, but decided to dilute the paint he used, so he could make a greater profit – at the church's expense. He started on the steeple. When he was about half way done, it began to rain. The thinned paint was now thinner still! But he kept right on. Suddenly out of the dark cloud there was a voice that cried: "Repaint! Repaint, and thin no more!"
     (**Message:** God calls us to turn from our sins. See Ezekiel 18:30b)

*****

103. Heaven
A florist in Kansas City was happy when she got a number of orders for

flowers to be delivered to a business that had relocated. The owner was pleased when he received the flowers, but there was one problem. One of the bouquets said: "Rest in Peace!" So, he called the florist to explain that a mistake must have been made. "Oh my goodness!" gasped the florist, "there's a funeral spray down at Oak Lawn that reads: 'Good luck in your new location!'"

(**Message:** Good luck is not necessary to get to Heaven, for we have a risen Savior! See John 14:1ff)

*****

104. Critics
He was a new hunting dog. The farmer who purchased him wanted a good retriever, and this dog proved to be the best! When he took him duck hunting, instead of swimming out to get the downed birds, this dog walked on top of the water! His owner could not believe his eyes!

Wanting to show him off, he invited his neighbor over to hunt on his large pond. The neighbor got the first bird, and true to form the farmer's dog walked across the surface of the pond, got the bird and returned. The neighbor did not comment! "Did you notice anything strange about my dog?" asked the owner. "Yes," he said, "He can't swim!"

(**Message:** Criticism comes cheap! Praise of another's blessings, comes from saints.)

*****

105. Mothers
I received the nicest note the other day. I will not share it all with you, but only the part that meant so much to me. "I believe that you are one of the finest preachers in America today. Furthermore, you are a very caring and sensitive man. The church is fortunate to have you." Signed, "Mother"

(**Message:** The perspective of a mother is different from that of the world!)

*****

106. Marriage
They had finally retired. He went for his annual physical, and she went

along with him, because her Jim had a hearing difficulty. After the exam, the doctor had them come into his office. There he explained that if Jim wanted to live to a ripe old age he was going to have to do three things.

First, he needed to cut back on fats and sweets in his diet. Second, he should walk a mile three times a week. Third, the doctor wanted him to be intimate with his wife twice a week. Then he explained that studies have shown that these three things were important if he was going to live a long life.

On the way home, Jim asked his wife what the doctor said. She said: "Jim! The doctor said you were going to DIE!"
     (**Message:** A good, fulfilling marriage involves several things. One of these is intimacy.)

*****

107. Marriage
The preacher was teaching the adult Sunday School Class. They were studying about King Solomon. The pastor stated that Solomon had 700 wives and 300 concubines. He added that the king fed his women a diet including ambrosia. Unimpressed, a little old man on the back row shouted out: "Never mind what he fed *them*, what did *he* eat?"
     (**Message:** The ingredients to a good marriage involve: commitment, communication, laughter...)

*****

108. Courage
A Texas oil well caught fire. The company called on some experts for help. They flew in, but could not get within 100 yards of the fire, so they gave up.

In desperation, the management called the local volunteer fire department to see if there was anything they could do. Fifteen minutes later their one loan fire truck managed to arrive on the scene. They drove right up to within *50 feet* of the fire! The five men on board jumped out, quickly sprayed down each other, then went to work on the flames. In fifteen minutes they had the fire extinguished!

In gratitude the company had a dinner in honor of the courageous firemen. After extolling their dedication and bravery, the president of the company presented the fire chief with a check for $10,000 for the department. Then he asked him what they were going to do with the money. The chief said: "Well, first I'm going to take the fire engine to the garage, and get those damned brakes fixed!"

(**Marriage:** Courage is a mixture of moving ahead against great odds while you are scared to death!)

*****

109. Appearances
C.M. Chandler of Rawlings, Wyoming tells how several years ago the state of Wyoming was paralyzed by a frigid winter with unheard of amounts of snow! So, the governor organized a hay lift to take bales of hay to stranded animals by way of aircraft.

One rancher was out in his-four-wheel drive pickup when he got stuck in a big drift. There was nothing to do, but walk the quarter of a mile back home. So, he put on his long bear skin coat, and started out. In a few minutes there was the sound of an airplane. Then a C-47 swooped in and dropped one bale of hay to the lonely fur-clad figure.

(**Message:** Things are not always to be identified by appearances. A Christian, the scripture declares, is known by his/her love! John 13:34-35)

*****

110. Parenting – or – Patience
The young husband was caught off guard one Sunday morning when his wife handed him the children's clothes, and then announced: "Here, *you* get the boys ready for church. I'm going out and honk the horn!"

(**Message:** We learn to appreciate our spouse sometimes when we stand in her/his shoes.)

*****

111. Patience
She had been sitting in the doctor's waiting room for over an hour. Every chair was full. There were the typical, light-hearted conversations, then

silence fell across the room. Finally, an elderly gentleman over in the corner struggled to his feet, and announced: "Well, I believe I will just go home, and die a natural death!"

*****

112. Missing the Point – or – Interpretation
A family was on a trip to Kissimmee, Florida. As they approached the town there was a debate in the car about how the name of the town was pronounced. As businesses grew more prevalent, they knew that they were near the city limits. Finally, there it was, the sign announcing the city! So, when the father saw a pedestrian nearby, he screeched the car to a halt! As he gestured toward the sign, he called out: "Say, how do you pronounce that?" The man walked over to the car, leaned in, and with careful enunciation said: "Bur–ger – King!"
   (**Message:** Sometimes we miss the point of God's Word too.)

*****

113. Baptism
A pastor was preparing to baptize an infant. He asked: "What name is to be given this child?" The mother answered: "Randolph Christopher Morgan-Johnson." With that the pastor turned to his assistant, and said, "A little more water, please!"
   (**Message:** How precious to be a part of God claiming a child for His own! See Matthew 3:17)

*****

114. Creativity
Teenagers are infamous for being hard to get out of bed – especially after a late night out. But one mother tops them all in her technique for getting her teenager awake and out of bed.

Her son sleeps with his dog. So, when she wants to get him up, she opens his bedroom door and throws their cat on the bed!
   (**Message:** There is more than one way to "skin a cat" as my father would say! i.e. Get the job done.)

115. Words – or – Humbling Experience
While serving in Kansas City I was the guest preacher at a downtown church. I was preaching on the raising of Lazarus, and how our Lord called him to come out of the tomb. To illustrate, I called out: "Lazarus! Lazarus!!" Suddenly from the basement of the church came a voice: "I'm coming! I'm coming!!" How was I to know that the custodian was named Lazarus?

(**Message:** There are times when you realize you have said the wrong thing!)

*****

116. Hypocrisy
Back in the 1800s train robbers went from car to car demanding the passengers' valuables. In the last car one of the robbers stuck his gun under the nose of a clergyman, and said: "Give me all your valuables!" (In those days the preacher could have raised his arms, and said: "If you find any, let me know!") The pastor said, "I am a man of God, you wouldn't rob me, would you?" The robber responded: "What kind of a preacher are you?" He said, "A Methodist." With that the robber extended his hand, and said: "Put it there, parson, I'm a Methodist too!"

(**Message:** "By this will all know you are my disciples," said our Lord, "By your love for one another!" John 13:35)

*****

117. Treasure
A group of salespersons and a group of Methodist clergy were holding conventions in the same large hotel. At mealtime the kitchen was a beehive of activity. Serving the two groups in separate dining rooms was no small task!

One evening the sales people had ordered spiked watermelon. However, amid the confusion it was delivered by mistake to the clergy. Suddenly, the chef realized the mistake. He called out to a waiter nearby: "Run out and see if the clergy are already eating the watermelon; if not bring it back!"

The waiter disappeared. A few minutes later he came running back empty-handed. "Well?" queried the worried chef. Breathless, the waiter finally was able to speak: "Sir, the clergy were already eating the watermelon." "Well, were they angry with us? What was going on?" asked the chef. "They were not saying much, but I did notice that a lot of them were putting the seeds in their pockets."

(**Message:** We know when we have got a good thing! The Gospel of Jesus Christ is the one *good* thing! Read: II Corinthians 4:7)

*****

118. Hope
It would be funny if it were not so sad; in March of 1996 a group of atheists in San Diego got permission from the city to have an Easter sunrise service in a city park. Think of it! What would they sing? To whom would they pray? What would their message of hope be? What would they say to those hungry for meaning to life? Think of the haunting silence …

(**Message:** God always gets the last word! – Revelation 21:6; "If for this life only we have hoped…We are of all persons most to be pitied!" I Corinthians 15:19)

*****

119. Marriage
After the pastor's sermon on marriage, Mike determined that he was going to work harder at being a more thoughtful, caring husband. So, on the way to work, he went by the florist shop and ordered a dozen roses. He was able to leave work a little early that day. He went by, picked up the roses, and headed for home. He walked in. Extended the roses to his wife, and said tenderly, "Honey, I love you!" But with that she burst into tears! "What a day!" she groaned, "Jimmy fell at pre-school and got a bad cut on his leg. I had a flat tire on the way home. Now you come home *drunk*!"

(**Message:** Marriage is not something that happens one day in June. It is a lifetime of patience, forgiveness, understanding and commitment to the one we love. – I Corinthians 13)

*****

120. Hypocrites
I preached at a small church one time that did not have a public address

system. I was not particularly concerned about being heard, for it was a small sanctuary. But before the service began the lay leader told me: "Brother Moore, you will need to speak loud, because this church has very bad *agnostics*."

(**Message:** The Church also has some agnostics too – persons who believe there is a God, but He really does not matter.)

*****

121. Protection or Fools for Christ

Back in the early 1980s I was invited to participate in a "We Care Mission in Buffalo, Missouri. The pastor of the church, Frederick Zahn, invited six of us for the three days of visitation and worship. During the daytime we were to visit all the local members of the church, and in the evening share our testimonies. It was a unique approach to revival in the church.

On the second day I got my list of visits to be made, and started out. I went down a country road to a farm house where some members lived. I pulled into the driveway while looking to see if there was a dog. I am not particularly afraid of dogs, but I have met my share that would love to drag you out back and bury you like a favorite bone!

I got out of the car, and "something" told me: "There is a dog here! Watch out!" I walked all the way to the front porch, and still no dog. Now I was beginning to rest easier following my attack of paranoia.

I knocked on the door, and I could hear him coming! Barking ferociously as he bounded around the corner of the house. It was a 100+ pound Pit Bull with massive chest and bigger jaws – so it seemed. Fortunately, the woman of the house was home, and opened the door. Immediately I dove in while introducing myself! We had a short visit wherein I told her about the "We Care Mission." Then it came time to face the dog!

I told her I was not sure about her dog – which was a lie, for I knew he wanted to kill and eat me! She assured me that he was friendly – that he *liked* men in particular. (I figured she meant: Like you "like" hamburger.) Nevertheless she offered to walk me to the car, which I readily accepted!

Hardly had we left the front porch before he raced around the house, and made a beeline for the preacher man – me! With the adrenalin pumping, I grabbed hold of this woman's arm – a woman who fifteen minutes before was a total stranger! I figured I could time it just right. I would throw her to the lions like any good pastor would do, while I jumped into the air, and moved forward at the same time. The first pass worked as planned. The dog flew by or under me, I do not know! But now he was sliding out into the yard on his side as he spun around for another attack. Together we did the old "two step" toward the car, then I would either leap into the air, or throw this poor little woman in front of the dog. Which only served to rile the dog up – I thought in hindsight! This was repeated about a dozen times, and God – working overtime – spared me from the jaws of the lion!

Finally, I arrived at my car door. Flung it open, and as the dog dove under the door for a juicy ankle bone, I leaped feet first into the car. How, I know not! I slammed the car door. Now I could see the poor disheveled woman standing wearily in the driveway – one arm longer than the other!

It was then that I rolled down the window a couple of inches and called out: "I do hope you will come to the service tonight." She said something that was inaudible – which was probably best, as I drove away thanking God for saving this modern day Daniel from the lion's den!
    (**Message:** God protects even fools who seek to do his work. – II Corinthians 4:7-11)

*****

122. Dog Tired – Need Rest
A woman took their ailing dog to the veterinarian. The dog just wanted to sleep all the time. The vet examined the "lifeless" pet as best he could. "I have one more procedure I would like to perform, if I have your permission," said the vet. The owner agreed.

The vet disappeared from the room, and moments later he brought in a black lab, and walked him round the sleeping dog. No response. Next he brought in this huge tomcat. Holding it by the back of neck, and down by its tail, he ran it up and down the dog. No response! Explaining that he knew nothing else to do, he explained that she should let the dog rest. She went to pay the bill. It was $350! She was aghast! So, the receptionist explained: "$50 is for the office visit. The lab test was $100, and the cat scan $200."

(**Message:** Things are not what they seem sometimes!)

*****

123. Marriage
A District Superintendent with the United Methodist Church in New England received a message on his answering machine one Friday evening. It said, "My wife just died. Please send a substitute for the weekend."

(**Message:** There is no substitute for a Christian marriage.)

*****

124. Comfortably Full
The Reverend Dr. Robert Arbaugh shares that we hear it said, "The church is comfortably full." He asked, "Bill, you do know what 'comfortably full' is, don't you? It is when there is room for a person to lie down between each worshipper."

(**Application:** We have probably all worshipped when the sanctuary was "comfortably full.")

*****

125. Lucky Day – or – Interpretation
A gentleman "down on his luck" knocked at the door. The woman answered. He said, "I have lost my job and need some help." "Can you paint?" she asked. "Yes, I painted a house once," he replied. "Well, I have a gallon of paint in the garage, and I have been wanting someone to paint the porch out back. I'll pay you what it is worth." She got him the paint, and he disappeared around the side of the house to start his work.

A little over an hour later, he was back at the door. "All finished," he said. Then added, "But lady! That's not a *Porsche* back there, that's a *Mercedes*!"

(**Message:** Just when you thought it was your lucky day, you realize that "luck" is a poor god to count on!)

126. Fear
She called the builder of their new home, and explained that when the train passed about three blocks from the house at 5:00 a.m., it nearly shook them out of bed! The builder thought she was surely exaggerating, but came by that afternoon to see if there was a problem.

He rang the doorbell. She welcomed him. Then she noticed that it was almost 4:00 p.m., and the Amrack was due. So, she said, "Come back here, and I will show you!" He followed her down the hall to the master bedroom. She said, "I hear the train coming, so lie down on the bed, and see what I am talking about!"

Well, it was not the train. It was the garage door. Her husband was home! When he saw the builder lying on the bed, he demanded an explanation. The terrified builder responded with trembling voice: "Would you believe I'm waiting for a train?"

    (**Message:** There are two types of fear: that based on imagined foes, and that based on reality!)

*****

127. Difficulties
Young James joined the paratroops. As the men were preparing for their first jump, the instructor explained once again that they were to count to ten, and then pull the cord. Then he explained further that if the chute fails to open, they were to pull the second cord to deploy a reserve chute. He added, "There will be a truck waiting to bring you back to the barracks."

They climbed aboard the plane, and soon were at the altitude for their jump. The men were lined up ready for their commander to give the order. Then, one-after-another they bailed out of the plane. When it came his turn, James followed. After counting to ten, he pulled the cord, and nothing happened. Remembering what the instructor had said, he pulled the second cord. Still, no chute was deployed. "Now," he said, "I'll bet that truck isn't there to pick us up either!"

    (**Message:** Difficulties! There are times when it seems everything is going wrong! – See Romans 8:38-39)

128. Unbelievable or Power
An old fellow from back in the hills came to the Atlanta airport to inquire about a ticket to New Orleans. He had never been to an airport, and the terminal was the largest building he had ever been in. By asking various persons, he was able to find the ticket counter he was looking for. The agent explained that they happened to have a seat on a flight that would leave at 9:25 and arrive in New Orleans at 9:30. He, not knowing about the difference in time zones, could not believe his ears!

Noting his hesitancy, the agent asked if he wanted a ticket? He said, "Nope! But I sure want to stick around to see that son-of-a-gun take off!"
      (**Message:** Some things in life seem unbelievable – such as how God could create us with all of the intricate systems that must be coordinated in the human body for it to work as it does.)

*****

129. Commitment
She meant *affiliated*, but that is not how it came out. I was new at the church, and one day I met a woman that I did not know. She spoke, so I asked: "Are you a member of the church?" "Oh yes," she gushed, "We have been afflicted with that church all our lives!"
(Message: A few members feel afflicted by the church when asked to give. Amazingly, they think that following the Crucified One is free!)

*****

130. Criticism
An elderly woman was buying stamps at the Post Office. She asked the clerk waiting on her if he would mind addressing an envelope. The clerk graciously obliged. Then he asked, "Is there anything else I can do for you?" "Yes, there is," she said, "If you don't mind write a note to go in it." She told him what to write, and he did so. Finally, he asked: "Anything else?" She said, "Yes, would you mind putting at the bottom: 'Please excuse this poor handwriting.'"
      (**Message:** A grateful heart is what puts joy in living! Sad the person who lacks that.)

131. Assurance

A little boy wrote a letter to God: "Dear God, how do you feel about persons who *don't* believe in you?" He signed his name, then added a postscript: "Somebody else wants to know!"

>(**Message:** Faith is not certainty. That comes from walking with Him and talking with Him. Read: II Timothy 1:12b)

*****

132. Atonement

Tony was on trial for having stolen $500 in postage stamps from his former employer. He hired a fine lawyer for his defense. In the end he was exonerated.

After the verdict, Tony hugged and thanked his attorney. "How can I ever repay you," Tony cried. "Just pay me my fee," said his attorney. "It is $2,500." "But," he added, "If you are pressed for cash right now you can pay me $500 a month." Tony responded: "I can't pay you in cash, but will you accept stamps?"

>(**Message:** We want to make right the wrongs we have done, but ultimately we must each depend on the mercy of God! See Colossians 2:13-14)

*****

133. Conversion – or – Influence

A rabbi took great pride in one Jewish boy in his congregation. In fact he envisioned him becoming a rabbi himself someday. But, when he grew up, the young man decided to go to Notre Dame. His rabbi encouraged him to watch lest someone try to convert him.

Over the winter break, the rabbi saw the young man. "They aren't trying to make a Roman Catholic out of you, are they?" he asked. His answer: "No, Father."

>(**Message:** We are influenced ever so subtly through the peers we identify with.)

*****

134. Salvation
A preacher died and went to Heaven. There he discovered scores of New York City taxi cab drivers, and very few clergy. He got St. Peter aside and asked what was going on? St. Peter explained it this way: "While the preachers preached, the sinners slept." "But the taxi drivers? They scared the Hell out of people!"

    (**Message:** People enter the Kingdom of God in different ways. Those who come out of fear will do only what is necessary to appease an angry God. But, glorious it is when one comes because she/he is simply overwhelmed with the love of God – they cannot do enough for their Savior!)

*****

135. Witnessing
One of my father's favorite stories involved a good friend of his, Bill Odom, who was an insurance salesman. Bill got a call one day from a woman who wanted information about some insurance. Eager to help her out, he offered to bring the information by her house the following morning.

He went to the address given which was in the black community. He knocked at the door, and an older woman answered. He said he was looking for a Miss Barbara Johnson. "Yes," she said, "She's my daughter. She can't come to the door, for she is taking a bath." Without thinking, Bill said, "I sure would like to see her!" To which the mother replied, "I'll bet you would, white boy!"

    (**Message:** Some Greeks came to Philip, and said, "Sir, we wish to see Jesus!" John 12:21b. THAT is the One the world hungers to see in you and me!)

*****

136. Love in the Home
The story is told of a Vermont man who lived with his wife for twenty-six years without ever telling her what he thought of her. Finally, one day he broke his silence. "Alice," he said, "When I get to thinking of how much you mean to me, it is almost more than I can do to keep from telling you!"

    (**Message:** Love that is not expressed regularly is greatly lacking!)

137. Transformation

Years ago a man from down in the hills attended an agricultural convention in a large hotel in Chicago. He had never been out of the county where he was born, so being in a large city was all new to him. While waiting his turn to register, he observed his first elevator. He did not know what it was!

About that time, and elderly woman came into the lobby. She made her way toward the elevator, shuffling her feet as she went. She pushed the button beside the door, and soon it opened. She stepped in, and the door closed. Then he watched as above the door numbers lit up. It went up to twenty-two, then reversed. When it arrived back at the lobby, the door opened. Out stepped this beautiful woman who must have been about twenty-two years old!

"Jumping Jehoshaphat!" he said, "Let me go home and get Momma, and put her in that thing!"
     (**Message:** Only the transforming power of Jesus Christ can make us new! – Philippians 3:20-21)

*****

138. Embarrassment

A preacher was invited to preach in Boston in an old formal church. On the appointed Sunday he was given a flowery introduction, after which he began to climb the steps up to the elevated pulpit. He was being careful to not step on his robe as he ascended. As he arrived at the pulpit, he acknowledged the crowd's continuing applause, stepped back a little too far, and plummeted end-over-end back down the steps landing on the keyboard of the grand piano with a mighty crash!

Getting to his feet he looked into the eyes of the horrified host pastor, and murmured: "Please don't tell anyone!"
     (**Message:** Sometimes it is too late to cover our bungling mistakes!)

*****

139. Potential / Children

A father, wanting to prod his son to seek to reach his fullest potential, said to him: "Son, you know what Abraham Lincoln was doing when he was your age, don't you?" "No," said the boy thoughtfully, "But I do know what he was doing at *your* age, Dad."

(**Message:** Just as we want our children to have better lives materially than we had, so, more importantly, we want them to attain a higher level of spirituality than we have.)

*****

140. Value of Knowledge
From Russia comes the story of the bird that lay along a path in the dead of winter. The bird was freezing! A peasant happened by, saw the bird, and was moved with compassion for it. He thought: "If only I had something warm to wrap this poor bird in, I might save its life." He had no clothing that he could spare, but then he saw some cow dung steaming in the frigid air. In desperation, he picked up the bird, and placed it in the manure mounding it up over its back. Sure enough the bird began to revive! It even began to give forth a croaky warble. The peasant went on his way.

Soon another peasant happened by. He heard the poor bird trying to sing. Saw that it was covered in dung, so he lifted it out of the muck, and placed it beside the path, and left. The bird froze to death.

There are three morals here: First, it is not necessarily your enemies who put you in it! Second, it is not necessarily your friends who get you out of it. Finally, when you are up to your chin in it, for heaven's sakes don't try to sing!

(**Message:** Sometimes acts of selfless love prove to be harmful. We need knowledge also to know what is best!)

*****

141. Ecumenicity
She was working toward full ordination in the United Methodist Church. But, just starting out, she knew she was not supposed to serve Holy Communion. So, when a Baptist in the small town died, and his church did not have a pastor, the family turned to the Methodist pastor.

Not knowing if she could do the funeral, she called the bishop. The bishop's response: "Sure! Bury all the Baptists you can!"

  (**Message:** First of all the above story did not happen! It illustrates the fun we can have with each other as Christians in spite of our differences!)

*****

142. Each is Precious
The young daughter of William Howard Taft III was assigned in her third grade class to write a short autobiography. She wrote simply: "My great grandfather was President of the United States from 1909 through 1913. My grandfather, Robert Alphonso Taft was senator from Ohio from 1949 through 1950. My father is an Ambassador to Ireland, and I'm a Brownie Scout."

  (**Message:** Each of us is a precious creation – in God's sight! – Psalm 8:5)

*****

143. The Cure
A sailor limped into the Naval Dispensary, had his foot x-rayed, and sat down to await the results. After a while a corpsman appeared in the doorway with a large white pill in his hand. Immediately an emergency was sounded, so before he rushed from the room, he handed the pill to the sailor saying: "Here, take this, and I will be back." With pill in hand, the sailor limped over to the sink, got a glass, and managed to swallow the pill.

Soon the corpsman returned with a bucket of warm water. "Okay," he said, "Drop the pill in the bucket, and we will soak that foot!"

  (**Message:** The cure is not what we usually think it is. We think material things can satisfy, but discover it is spiritual things that are the answer.

*****

144. Unbelievable
A Roman Catholic nun was traveling out in the open expanses of western Texas when she ran out of gas. About a mile down the road, she could

see a gas station, so she decided to walk to it. When she arrived, she was told that the only gas can the attendant had was gone. Well, he did sell antiques on the side, and remembered that he had just purchased a chamber pot. It was in the back of his car. Knowing that he could trust the nun with its return, he got it, put a half gallon of gas in it, and gave it to her along with a funnel. He explained, "I would take you to your car, sister, but I am the only one here to attend to the station."

She took the chamber pot with the gas and the funnel, and headed toward her car. With the funnel in place, she tilted the chamber pot, and began pouring the fuel. It was then that a trucker happened by. He screeched his rig to a halt, and called down to the nun: "My goodness, Sister! You sure have a lot more faith than I do!"

(**Message:** Faith is required oftentimes to see the greatness of God! – See Luke 17:6)

*****

145. Persistence

Mary bought a parrot. She placed it in its cage in the corner of the kitchen so that every time she came by the cage she would say, "Hello," and thereby teach the bird to talk. Several times each day she would repeat her routine, but the bird refused to speak!

After a couple of weeks her patience ran out. So, the next morning when she went into the kitchen for breakfast, she did not speak. With that the parrot said, "Well, well! And what's wrong with you this morning?"

(**Message:** The prize goes, not to the one who *starts* the race, but to the one who *finishes*! – See II Timothy 4:7-8)

*****

146. Sin

He was known for his waywardness around town. When the priest crossed the alley one morning, he saw him leaning against a building reading a newspaper. The priest spoke, and the man responded: "Say, Father! What can cause arthritis?" Seeing an opportunity for a teaching moment, the priest replied: "Drinking too much wine, gambling, and chasing women. Why did you ask?" "Because it says here in the paper that the Pope has arthritis."

(**Application:** "We ALL sin, and fall short…" Romans 3:23 – But sin is not what causes arthritis.)

*****

147. Hide from Sin
Father Anthony de Mello tells of a priest who was out for a stroll in his neighborhood, when he saw a small youngster trying to reach a doorbell. The priest thought he could help the little fellow out, so he walked up the sidewalk, and rang the bell. Suddenly, the youngster yelled, "Now, RUN!!"

(**Application:** Some of us have played: "Ring the doorbell, then run and hide." We cannot so easily hide from our sins as adults though!)

*****

148. Heaven
Small churches often rely on members to fix things. So, when the public address system went out in one small church, a member with some knowledge of electronics offered to try and fix it. He finally narrowed the problem down to a short in the wiring that ran from the amplifier to the speakers.

To solve this problem he got the speaker wire he needed, then climbed up in the crawl space above the sanctuary ceiling. His wife, worried that he might fall through the ceiling came along, and waited in a pew in the sanctuary below. As she waited, some visitors looking for a wedding chapel came by. Thinking that the lone soul in the sanctuary was praying, they decided to wait in the narthex for her to finish. But were shocked when the dear woman rose to her feet, and looking heavenward, she cried out: "Bob! Bob!! Did you make it?" The sympathy of the witnesses to all this, changed to laughter when Bob answered: "Yes, honey, I made it just fine!"

(**Application:** On the Mount of Transfiguration, three of the disciples witnessed the heavenly beings: Moses and Elijah, who appeared and talked with the Lord." Mark 9:2-8 Yes! We will know and be known there!)

*****

149. Fear / All Sin

In the 1840s in the mountains of eastern Kentucky, a bishop came to preside over the trial of a pastor charged with using profanity – an offense that, in those days, could get a person thrown out of the ministry. The bishop made it clear that the only way the proceedings could move forward was if there was a person who actually heard the pastor use the profanity. Well, a man testified that he heard the defendant use an oath. So, the bishop allowed him to proceed with his account.

"It was at the funeral of Sister Elviry," he said. "She was all stove up with arthritis to the point that she was bent over. So, the undertaker had to tie her down in the casket."

In the middle of the parson's message the cord broke, and Sister Elviry sat up! The bishop interrupted, "Is that when you heard the pastor use the profanity?" "No," he went on, "It was about 30 seconds later – about a quarter of a mile from the church – when the parson passed me with a window frame around his neck. It was then I heard him say: 'These damned one-door churches!' "

(**Message:** The bishop understood, and dismissed the charge!)

*****

150. Temptation

Someone has said that there are three ways to get something done. The first is to do it yourself. The second is to hire it done. The third is to tell your children that they cannot do it. *That* is the surest way of getting it done!

(**Message:** Temptation! God's Word says it is Common. It is Conditioned. It is Conquerable! See this in: I Corinthians 10:13)

*****

151. Long Life

Years ago "Carter's Little Liver Pills" were popular to take for their health benefits. The creator of the pills impressed on potential customers the importance of keeping one's liver healthy, and that his pills were designed to do just that!

One man took the pills for 40 years, and finally died at age 92. The only problem: they had to beat his liver to death with a stick!

   (**Message:** We all wish for a long and healthy life, but far greater is eternal life in Christ Jesus!)

*****

152. Giving

The church needed a new organ. The organist was especially eager to see the project be a success. So, on the Sunday that the pastor made the appeal for funds, she said: "All who will give $500 toward the new organ please stand." Suddenly the organist began playing the "Star Spangled Banner!"

   (**Message:** We should not have to be tricked into giving. To be a follower of the Crucified Savior means being a sacrificial giver!)

*****

153. Giving

An elderly miser had kept all of his money to himself. He had not learned, in all his years of life, the joy of giving!

Well, one evening as he was out for a stroll, two thieves attacked him. Instead of giving in, he fought back, and with surprising fury! In fact he was about to whip both of the young men, when one of them snatched up four quarters that had fallen from their victim's pocket as they ran away. Wiping blood from their faces as they went, one said to the other: "If that old man would have had five dollars in his pocket, he would have killed us both!"

   (**Message:** We rejoice at a story of a person getting the upper hand on a thief, but greater still is the blessing of giving, that gives us an upper hand on the doldrums of life! – See Luke 6:38)

*****

154. Ecumenicity

Patrick Hooley had a small store in Minneapolis, a city of largely Norwegian Lutherans. Patrick, an Irish Catholic, was surprised when he was encouraged to run for alderman, and even more surprised when he won! In time, the same community recommended that he run for mayor. Again, they got behind him, and he was elected!

A Lutheran pastor even asked the new mayor to speak at an intermission of a cantata at the church. Mayor Hooley said, "Only in America could an Irish Catholic be elected mayor in a largely Norwegian Lutheran city! But who could have expected your choir to sing for me today: 'Hooley, Hooley, Hooley, Lord God almighty!'"

    (**Message:** It is great when we as Christians can look beyond denominational differences!)

*****

155. Challenges
A pastor in a liturgical church usually opened worship with the blessing: "The Lord be with you." The congregation then responded: "And also with you."

One Sunday morning there was a problem with the public address system. (Imagine that!) The light that usually came on when he turned his microphone on did not light up, so he knew the mike was dead. As he wrestled with it, he said, "This mike is not working." The congregation responded: "And also with you!"

    (**Message:** Paul had his ship wrecks. Pastors today have PA systems!)

*****

156. Joyful Blunders
A pastor in our Conference, told a story about the year he planned a New Year's Eve celebration that started at 7:30 p.m., and went until midnight. There were various singing groups, testimonies, and a "hymn-sing." Then at one minute until midnight he announced solemnly: "Let us now bow in prayer as another Dear is Yawning!" That year they "laughed in" the New Year!

    (**Message:** What better way to bring in the New Year as Christians!)

*****

157. Guilt / Pain

One clergy friend asked: "Do you know what happens when you play a country recording backwards? – You get your dog back; your gun back; your pick-up back; and your wife back!"

    (**Message:** When we live life backward we focus on guilt and pain, but God declares: "THIS is the Day the Lord has made. Let us rejoice, and be glad in it!!" – Psalm 118:24 – Every day is Easter Day for the Christian!)

*****

158. Changed – or – Parenting

On the wall of a church nursery I saw this biblical quotation: "We shall not all sleep, but we shall all be changed." – I Corinthians 15:51

    (**Message:** Living in Christ brings change – We are changed into His likeness. Lord, make it so!)

*****

159. Trials

It was a cold day, and two Catholic nuns, attired in their habits, were waiting out in front of the employment office for a bus. Realizing that it would be a while before the bus came, a worker went out and invited the sisters to come in for a hot cup of coffee. They were very grateful for the woman's kindness, and followed her in.

About that time two fellows who were looking for work came in. When they saw the nuns, one said to the other: "If even the Pope is laying them off – we are in trouble!"

    (**Message:** Things could always be worse!)

*****

160. Blessings/Trials

A commuter boarded a train in New York. He told the conductor that he was going to Fordham. The conductor explained that they did not stop in Fordham on Saturdays, but offered a solution: "We always slow down for Fordham, so when we do, I'll open the door, and you can jump off. But remember you must hit the ground running in the direction the train is moving, or you will take a tumble!"

As the train approached Fordham, the train began to slow. The conductor, who had apparently had experience with this, opened the door and at the right moment yelled: "Jump!" The passenger did. As he hit the ground he began running with the train. An alert conductor in the car behind saw the man running beside the train, so he reached out, caught him by the arm, and pulled the little fellow on board – once again! Before the breathless man could speak, he said, "This is your lucky day! The train does not stop at Fordham on Saturdays!"

    (**Message:** Sometimes our lucky day is not so "lucky." In fact a good day is a "blessed day" – blessed, not by "luck," but by the Lord!

*****

161. Giving
The Finance Committee was meeting. The need for a new organ was being discussed. Someone mentioned that they had priced them, and they were right at $100,000. One gentleman, who had a flair for calling attention to himself but not producing much, looked the members over, finally he said: "I will match anything that any one of the rest of you give." With that an elderly widow announced: "Sonny, you and I just bought a new organ!"

    (**Message:** Jesus did not say: "IF you give," but "WHEN you give" – Matthew 6:2 – See also verses: 19-21 & 24)

*****

162. Missing Out
Some American tourists flew to London for a tour of England. One day the tour bus took them to Runnymede. The guide explained that it was here that the Magna Carta was signed. One man asked: "When?" The guide said: "1215." The tourist looked at his watch, and said: "Heck! We just missed it by thirty minutes!"

    (**Application:** There are some things you do not want to miss out on...)

*****

163. Detours

A cowboy was out riding his horse. He was feeling pretty cocky when he happened on an old prospector with his mule in tow. He rode up beside him, and said: "Old man, would you like to dance?" With that he pulled his rifle from its scabbard, and began shooting near the fellow's feet. Of course he danced about, trying to keep from getting hit. But finally the gun was empty. Whereupon the prospector pulled out a gun, and said, "Young man, would you like to kiss my mule?" "No," said the cowboy, "but I will!"

(**Application:** There are many times in life when God calls upon us to do something we are reluctant to do: help the poor, extend a hand to our enemy, preach the Gospel, teach the Gospel, and the list goes on! Acts 16:6-10 tells of a time Paul was prevented from doing what he had planned, so that he would do what the Lord had planned for him to do!)

*****

164. The Way

While attending a retreat one fall at Lake Louise in Alberta, Canada, an associate of the Billy Graham Association shared a story about a Chicago crusade that Dr. Billy Graham conducted early in his ministry. Needing to get some stamps to mail a few letters, Dr. Graham left the hotel to find a Post Office. A couple of blocks down the street he asked a boy he met for directions. The lad pointed the way, then Billy added: "You probably don't know who I am. I am Billy Graham. Come tonight to our service, and I will tell you how to get to Heaven." Unimpressed, the lad responded: "You kidding? Why you don't even know how to get to the Post Office!"

(**Message:** The first Christians were called "followers of the Way" before being named "Christians.")

*****

165. Temptation

A Los Angeles school teacher had been teaching her second grade class some Proverbs. To review, she asked: "Cleanliness is next to what?" A little boy answered: "Impossible!"

Jimmy was reluctantly getting ready to go to church. "Why do I have to go to church? – I already know how to be a nicer boy than I want to be!"

(**Message:** The above two illustrations point out the difficulty temptation causes us. I Corinthians 10:13 points the way out!)

*****

166. Sinners

The Reverend Anthony deMello, S.J. tells of a man who was looking for a church to attend. Having lived a very rough life, he was looking for a new beginning! He visited several churches, but they just were not what he was looking for.

One Sunday he attended an Episcopalian Church. The service had already begun when he arrived. The congregation was praying in unison, out of the Book of Common Prayer, "We have left undone those things which we ought to have done, and have done those things which we ought not to have done…" With that he sank into a seat and said, "I have found my kind of folks!"

(**Message:** The Church is a hospital for sinners, NOT a museum for the display of saints! Every church door ought to have a sign above the door that reads: "For Sinners Only!")

*****

167. Stress

The frantic new father called 911 to get an ambulance. "My wife is pregnant, and her contractions are only 5 minutes apart!" The operator calmly asked: "Is this her first child?" "NO! You fool!" shouted the man, "This is her *husband*!"

(**Application:** Stress is the tension that keeps life going. Managing stress is a secret that is as vital as it is ambiguous! As a Christian, it is critical to remember Who you are grounded in! John 15:5)

*****

168. Parenting

A parent once told me: "Our six year old son just got a dog. So, we are sending him to obedience school. If it works out, we will send the dog too!"

(**Message:** Learning to say, "No" to ourselves is an important lesson to learn early. For it will save us in adulthood from becoming slaves of our passions, lusts, and appetites. He/she is freest who has learned to discipline himself/herself!)

*****

169. Speeches
A pastor friend told me about being invited back to his home town to bring the address at a special 4th of July Celebration. When the appointed hour arrived, the town dignitaries gathered on the platform. A decorated veteran was the master of ceremonies. Finally, he introduced my friend, and then added: "The men in uniform will fire a salute over those who are dead after the address."

(**Message:** You only hope folks will not die while waiting for your speech to finish!)

*****

170. Hospitality
A woman in Phoenix tells of going home to a small town in North Dakota for a special homecoming. It was a town small enough that everyone knew everyone else. They gathered in the Dime Store on Main Street to reminisce.

A man walked into the store. He looked familiar, so she ran up and gave him a big hug, then said, "Your face is familiar. Tell me your name!" "Well," said the guy with a startled look, "I am driving through to California. Boyee, this SURE is a FRIENDLY town!"

(**Message:** Our Lord taught us to welcome the stranger in our midst! – Matthew 25:35ff)

*****

171. Patience / Stamina
A new pastor was being led around the church by one of the old patriarchs. As they were looking over the Pastor's Study, he said: "Pastor, we have a long standing tradition here of allowing the preacher to preach as long as he likes. But we leave at 12:00 sharp!"

(**Message:** Someone has said that a pastor's sermon is like a woman's dress. It needs to be long enough to cover the subject, but short enough to be of interest!)

*****

172. Obedience
A nineteenth century industrialist told Mark Twain: "Before I die I want to make a pilgrimage to the Holy Land. I will climb Mt. Sinai, where God gave the Ten Commandments to Moses. I want to stand there on the summit, and read the Commandments aloud.

Mark Twain said to him: "Sir, why don't you just stay right here in New York City, and keep them!"
(**Message:** It is easier to read the Bible than to obey its lessons of Love!)

*****

173. Rest
This parishioner called the church office, and asked for the pastor. She answered, and the voice on the other end of the line said: "I called for you yesterday, but they said you were not in." "I'm sorry," said the pastor, "But Monday is my day off." "Satan never takes a day off," came the curt reply. "That's right," said the pastor, "And if I never took a day off, I would be as mean as the devil too!"
(**Message:** Everyone needs time away. Even Jesus took time off! – See: Mark 6:31 – If you are to have the best from your pastor, *insist* that she/he take regular times away to rest!)

*****

174. Honesty
A woman purchased a used car. The next day she brought the car back. The salesman who sold it to her asked: "Is there a problem?" "Not at all," she said politely, "I just wanted to return the things that the little old lady who had this car before me overlooked when she sold the car. Here is a box of cigars and these size 12 running shoes I found in the trunk."
(**Message:** We pick on used car salespersons, but dishonesty can occasionally be found in all businesses.)

175. Honesty – or – Ethics

Years ago down in the Ozark hills a woman made a green bean pie, and took it by the parsonage. The pastor answered the door, thanked the woman for her thoughtfulness, and she left.

The next day they cut into the pie, and discovered the green beans. The taste of the pie had much to be desired! So, they fed it to the two family dogs.

Next Sunday the woman asked the pastor how he liked the pie. He answered, "Mabel, pies like that don't last long at our house!"

(**Message:** Love must be the bedrock guide in all things. The loving thing in this situation demanded that the pastor answer as he did. He was being literally honest, and at the same time considerate of the woman's feelings.)

*****

176. Grace

Mr. Johnson, suffering from chest pain, entered the emergency room of the hospital. He was whisked back to a room where a doctor began to order tests. Soon he was headed to surgery for heart blockages.

Later in the recovery room a Catholic nun, representing the hospital, announced: "Mr. Johnson, you are going to be just fine! But we will need to know the name of your insurance." "I don't have any," he said. "Can you make cash payments?" she queried. "I'm afraid I can't," he said. "Well, do you have any close relatives that might help you out?" "Just a sister who is a spinster nun," he added. "Nuns are *not* 'spinsters,'" she corrected, "They are married to God!" "Okay," smiled the man, "Send the bill to my Brother-in-law!"

(**Message:** We cannot pay our debt either! Thus, we must all fling ourselves on the mercy God in Christ!)

*****

177. Inadequacy of Preaching

The wife of a preacher in Kansas was afraid to fly. But, when her daughter in Florida sent her a round trip ticket to visit her, she decided to give it a try. As she was about to board the plane, she gave her pastor husband an envelope which read: "Open in case of a disaster."

After her husband returned home, he could not resist the temptation, so he opened the envelope anyway. Inside was a note which read: "If I do not return, look under the bed. You will find a box. Open it." Immediately he went and found the box – under the bed as she had said. He opened it, and was shocked to find three eggs, and a stack of $100 bills!

As soon as his wife arrived back home he admitted what he had done. Then he asked: "What is the meaning of the three eggs, and the bundle of $100 bills?" She explained: "Honey, when you started preaching, every time you 'laid an egg' by having a poor sermon, I would put an egg in the box under the bed.

"You mean," he interrupted, "In all these many years I only had three bad sermons?" What's this with the $100 bills?" "Well," she explained, "When you get a dozen, you gotta sell!"
    (**Message:** I had a seminary professor, who later became a bishop, who once said, "I've never heard a sermon that I didn't get something out of. But I have had some pretty close calls! Paul said it a little differently: (paraphrasing him) through the foolishness of what we preach, persons are saved. – See I Corinthians 1:21)

*****

178. Humility

A barber, who was always putting down everyone around him, was cutting this fellow's hair. The man told him that he was going to Italy. "What airlines are you going to fly on?" the barber asked. "Italia Airlines out of New York," he said. "Italia?" jeered the barber, "They have a terrible record! You better have your life insurance paid up if you fly with them. Where are you going to stay?" "The Hilton in Rome," the customer answered. "I hear that the Hilton in Rome is a real dump!" said the barber. "What are you going to see?" he asked. "I'm going to have an audience with the Pope." "The Pope won't see you," said the barber, "He only sees important people!"

Three weeks later, the man was back for a hair cut. "How was your trip?"

said that barber with a skeptical sneer. "Oh it was great! We flew over on Italia Airlines, and had a very smooth flight. We settled in at the Hilton, and had a wonderful stay." "Well, I guess you didn't get to see the Pope anyway." "Oh, yes," he said, "I got to see the Pope, and I even kissed his ring." "Well, what did he say to you?" "He looked down on the top of my head, and said, "Son, where on earth did you get that terrible haircut?"

(**Application:** If we do not possess humility in the present, we will in time be humbled. Humility is the gateway to the heart of God; the beginning point of prayer; the launching pad from which we rise into Life eternal in Christ Jesus! – I Peter 5:6 says, "Humble yourself under the mighty hand of God, that in due time He may exalt you."

*****

179. How is it with Your Soul?

A patrolman came upon an accident. A farmer had been thrown out of his overturned pickup truck, and was lying on one side of the road. His mule that had been in the back was lying on the other. The patrolman, realizing the poor condition of the mule, pulled out his revolver and put it out of its misery.

Then, he crossed the road. Without thinking, he had not yet returned his pistol to its holster. He explained to the farmer sitting in the ditch, "Your mule was in bad shape, so I had to shoot her." Then he added: "How are you?" The farmer said: "Just fine! Just fine!!"

(**Application:** We need often to reflect on: how is it with my soul? That is a question that early Methodists would ask each other weekly. An African was leading a group of tourists through the bush country. Come Sunday he made a place in the shade of a tree, and sat down. When asked what he was doing, he said: "I'm letting my soul catch up with my body." We all need that!)

*****

180. Fear / Courage

Mother asked five year old Timmy to get a can of tomato soup out of the pantry. Well, it was dark in there, and he was going through a stage of being afraid of the dark. Finally, he admitted that he was scared. Trying to reassure her son, she said, "Son, Jesus will be in there with you." Reluctantly he opened the pantry door. As he looked in to the darkness, he called out: "Jesus, would you hand me a can of tomato soup?"

(**Message:** God says to us, His children, "Fear not!" He says those words in scripture at least once for every day of the year. I think we get the idea!)

*****

181. Motivation – or – Trials
I read of a typographical error in an advertisement for a resort area in North Carolina that was known for its golf courses. The ad stated: "There are more golf curses per mile than anywhere in the world!"

Speaking of curses, a grandfather heard his granddaughter use the word "darn." He was from a straight-laced tradition that avoided such slang. So, he told her, "Honey, I will give you a dollar if you won't use that word again." She agreed, and received the dollar.

A week later, the little girl greeted her grandfather with: "Grandpa, I have a word that is worth five dollars!"

(**Message:** As Christians it is the Love of God in Christ that motivates us to do what is right. Romans 5:15)

*****

182. Attitudes
A woman was part of the jury pool being screened for an upcoming trial. "Your honor," she said to the judge, "I cannot serve, for I do not believe in capital punishment." "You don't understand Madam," the judge countered, "This trial involves a civil suit. A woman is asking to recover $10,000 of her money that her husband allegedly spent on gambling and other women." "Oh," she said, "I can serve. I could be wrong about capital punishment!"

(**Message:** Attitudes *can* be changed!)

*****

183. Persistence
Back in the days when radio was the means of mass communication, Bob Burns was a famous radio comedian. He used to tell how he grew

up eating mostly deep, fat, fried foods. When he entered the Army at 18, the bland G.I. grub cured him of a lifelong case of heartburn! In fact, he grew up thinking that the burning in his stomach and throat was a part of living!

He says, "I shall never forget the day I rushed down to the dispensary holding my stomach, and crying: "Doc, Doc! Help me, I'm dying! My fire has gone out!"

     (**Message:** Is your "fire" as a Christian growing or going – out? Paul could boast of how he: "finished the race, and kept the faith!" II Timothy 4:7b)

*****

184. Witnessing

The barber was a new Christian. He was excited about his newfound faith. So, he wanted to share it with others.

One day as he was stropping his razor in preparation for giving a fellow a shave, the thought came to him: "I need to witness about my faith to this guy." But he was not sure how to go about it, so he stalled as he sharpened his razor. Finally, he blurted out: "Sam, are you ready to meet your God?"

     (**Message:** Witnessing comes in many forms, but this is not one of them! Seriously, it is important that we *name* the Lord, for the world is aware of the blessings; they just think it is luck who provided them! – Ephesians 1:15-23, esp. verse 21b)

*****

185. Embarrassment

Grandmother was fixing lunch in the kitchen when her grandson came in. He announced: "I have been playing mailman." "How can you do that when you have no mail to deliver?" she asked. "Well, you know those old letters upstairs in the trunk with a ribbon tied around them? I put one of those in each of the mailboxes on this street."

(**Application:** There are some things in life that will make your heart skip a beat; this would be one!)

186. Count Your Blessings

He had not been to church in years. Instead he often spent his weekends at the race track. But, one Sunday he pleased his wife very much when he announced that he was going with her.

On the way home he announced: "That wasn't so bad! The pews were padded. The place was air conditioned, the pastor's speech was interesting, and the music was great!" His wife said, "Yes, honey, I was glad to see you go! It was good to hear you using your beautiful baritone voice to sing the hymns. But, next time remember it is '*Hallelujah* thine the glory,' not '*Hileah*…!'"

(**Application:** It is a true gift from God to be able to count our blessings, rather than focusing on the mistakes of others.)

*****

187. Paying for our Sins

A sailor, who had attended the Methodist Church since retiring from the Navy, died. His Will spelled out that his pet parrot was to go to the care of the pastor of the church. But soon the preacher learned that the bird could swear profusely! He tried everything to break the bird of its bad habit. He offered rewards, and punishment – but to no avail.

The Women's Group at the church had been scheduled to meet at the parsonage for a social gathering. The time for the event was drawing near! Thus, the pastor was getting desperate! The morning of the gathering the bird was showing no change in behavior. In fact he was more liable to spout forth a few curses when visitors came.

So, the pastor came up with a final plan. "The parrot is a tropical bird," he thought, "So he would not like cold weather. So the next time he swears, I will put him in the freezer for a while." He did not have to wait long, before the bird cut loose with an oath. He grabbed him out of his cage, and put him in the freezer.

After a few minutes he cracked open the door to the freezer, and said, "Are you going to quit cursing?" "Yeeeeessss," chattered the bird. So he took him out, and was carrying him back to his cage when the parrot asked: "Whaat – did – the tur-tur-turkey do?"

(**Message:** Bad habits are difficult to break! Yet, what is impossible for us, is possible for God! Romans 7:24-25)

*****

188. Forgiving
I am told that there is a sign on the wall of a convent in Maryland that reads: "No Trespassing! Trespassers will be prosecuted to the full extent of the law!" Signed: "Sisters of Mercy."
    (**Message:** Forgiving persons of their trespasses against us is difficult for all of us Christians. Yet, Jesus teaches us the importance of doing just that in Matthew 5:43-45)

*****

189. Love for Unlovely
There was a school teacher, a garbage collector, and the CEO of an HMO who came to the Pearly Gates. St. Peter informed them that they would have to answer a question in order to enter Heaven.

He first asked the teacher: "Name the famous passenger ship that hit the iceberg and sank." She said, "Titanic." St. Peter ushered her through the gate.

Then he turned to the garbage collector, and asked: "How many died: 1000, 1200, or 1500." He had seen the movie "Titanic," so he answered: "1500." St. Peter ushered him in. Then he came to the CEO of the HMO, and said, "Name them!"
    (**Application:** Right now it is popular to be angry with the wealthy health care providers. – Matthew 5:44)

*****

190. Own worst Enemy
Back in 1995 CNN interviewed Larry Walters, who wanted to fly, but who ended up stopping air traffic near the Los Angeles Airport. Larry was a truck driver who had always wanted to fly, but his eyesight was not up to par with the requirements of pilots, so he had been turned down.

One day Larry came up with the idea of flying in his lawn chair. He went down to the local Army Surplus Store, and rented a tank of helium, and purchased 40 weather balloons – the kind that measure four feet across when fully inflated!

Back home he anchored the chair with a rope to his car. Packed a lunch with drinks, and tied on a BB gun that he figured he could use to burst the balloons one-by-one, when he was ready to come down.

His plan was complete except for airing up the weather balloons. When he had filled enough balloons with the helium that he was convinced there was adequate lift, he sat down in his lawn chair, strapped himself in, then reached down and cut his tether loose from the automobile. Suddenly he was jerked skyward! He did not slowly drift into the heavens, as he had planned, but was catapulted into the sky at an increasing rate of speed!

By the time he thought of his BB gun, he didn't dare shoot out a balloon, for he was more than a thousand feet up, and climbing! He reached 11,000 feet before his ascent stopped, and he began to drift.

Controllers at LAX spotted him on their radar. Though they could not figure out what the object was, nevertheless they had to route air traffic around it.

So, he floated around in his lawn chair for over ten hours! Finally, a Pan Am pilot radioed that he just passed a man in a lawn chair at 11,000 feet! (Imagine the conversation in the Control Tower over that!)

He was rescued when an Air Force helicopter came, and managed to get him back on ground where he was arrested. A reporter asked: "What did you think of while you were up there?" He said, "I learned to pray!"
  (**Application:** Many of our trials are situations we bring upon ourselves. Often they bring us to see our need for God!)

*****

191. Eternal Life
The Social Security Administration sent out a computer-produced letter

which read: "Dear Mrs. Johnson, we have received word that you are deceased. Your Social Security payments will cease immediately. If your circumstances should change, you may reapply at our office."

(**Message:** Only those who know the Lord can make plans beyond death! – I Corinthians 15:19)

*****

192. Good News / Bad News
A woman went on a trip to Europe. Her husband stayed behind to look after Fluffy, the cat, and his mother-in-law. His wife called from London to see how things were going. "I'm sorry to tell you, dear," he said, "but Fluffy has died!" "That's no way to break such news to me when I am away," she scolded. "You should have said, 'Fluffy is on the roof, and I cannot get him down.' Then when I called back, later in the trip, you could tell me he was badly injured. Finally, when I called back a third time you could explain that Fluffy had died. That way the news wouldn't come as such a shock!" Her husband apologized for not thinking of that himself.

The next week his wife called from Paris. She asked how things were going. He said, "Honey, your mother is on the roof!"

(**Application:** Surprises! They can be good, and they can be bad. But, Paul says: "We know that in *everything* God works for good, with those who love Him…" Romans 8:28a)

*****

193. Christmas
What if there had been three "Wise Women," who had come from afar to find the Christ child. First, they would have asked for directions. Second, they would have gotten there *before* the Baby was born. Third, they would have helped deliver the Baby (a task for *all* Christians!). Finally, they would have brought practical gifts like diapers, clothes, and baby oil!

(**Message:** Beneath the angels heralding His birth, is the humble circumstances in which the Mighty God chose to become flesh among us! – Luke 2:15ff)

194. Fear

My wife, Ginya, tells a story of Mr. Short, a neighbor she had when she was growing up. Mr. Short had a farm. Part of his operation was raising chickens.

One night He heard a commotion in the chicken coop. His dog was barking ferociously, so he was sure that a fox must have gotten in.

As he was going out the door in his nightshirt, he grabbed his double-barreled shot gun. His dog followed him to the hen house. (Brave dog!) As he crept up to the door, a full moon lighted his way. He lifted his shotgun. Opened the door, and leaned in to see what was causing the bedlam. As he did, the dog's cold nose got him from behind, causing him to fire both barrels into the coop – killing twelve chickens! (There was no sign of an intruder!)

(**Message:** Think of it! Our fears have a way of realizing themselves. How many wars have been fought because nation states were fearful? It is also true on a personal level. If we worry enough about our health, we will have poor health!...– See Matthew 10:26-30)

*****

195. Answered Prayer / Guidance

Jim, who lived in New York, had a problem. So, one day he approached a coworker, who he felt he could trust, and shared his struggle to decide on bride. "I'm torn between Betty and Maria. Both are wonderful persons, and I would be happy with either one, but I cannot decide which to propose to! How do you Catholics make such a decision?" "I go to church," shared his friend, "I spend several minutes bowed in prayer, and when I look up the answer usually comes to me!"

So, the very next Sunday, Jim went with his friend to mass. He bowed in prayer for most of the service. Finally, as the priest was finishing his homily, he looked up. Sure enough, high above a stained glass window was his answer! He read: "ave Maria!"

(**Message:** God does not always answer in such a dramatic way – but He does *always* answer! If we but pray. I Kings 19:11-12)

*****

196. Does God Speak?
She had just turned four. On this night she did not want to go to bed because the room was dark. After three trips to her parents' bedroom, her father tried to reassure her by telling her: "Honey, you are not alone in your bedroom, God is with you."

Reluctantly, she returned to her bedroom. She stuck her head in the darkened room, and said: "God! If you are in here, *please* don't say anything! It will *scare* me to death!"

     (**Message:** In I Samuel 3:4f God calls to Samuel in the night, and he answered: "Here am I!" If we are but willing to do God's will and pray about it, God *will* reveal His will to us!)

*****

197. On Getting the Message
A passenger aboard a ship saw a bearded man on an island they were passing. The man was shouting and waving his arms in the air. The passenger asked a crewman: "Who is that guy?" The crewman said, "I have no idea. But every time we pass he goes mad!"

     (**Message:** The world is crying out for the Good News, but too often Christian people do not get the message, and simply pass them by!)

*****

198. Impression
Zelda Harrison was known throughout her 83 years as a very negative person. If the sun was shining – we needed rain instead. If it was rainy, she would announce: "Another gloomy day!" She had seen many changes in her life, and in her church, and she was against every one of them! Zelda was not a happy camper, and she made life miserable for those around her.

One August day Zelda died. Her funeral was planned in the little church where she had attended all her life. On the day of the funeral all the mourners were fanning away with the fans provided by, advertising Atchley Funeral Home. The pastor rose, and still trying to think of something good to say about Zelda without stretching the truth too far, approached the pulpit. Suddenly, there was a tremendous crash of thunder that shook the whole building! He simply paused, gave a sheepish grin, and announced: "Zelda has arrived!"

(**Application:** What impression will we leave on the minds of those who knew us best? – See Colossians 4:18)

*****

199. Greatness

It is said that Thomas Edison, after years of labor, finally got his first electric light bulb to give forth a glow! He was jubilant! His wife who was sleeping nearby was unaware of what he had done until he cried: "Dear! I have finally done it!!" She rolled over and said, "Will you turn that light out and come to bed!"

(**Application:** We all at times fail to realize that we are standing in the midst of greatness: a child shares a discovery, or accomplishment they have made. A new Christian shares the power of prayer they have just discovered...)

*****

200. Holy amid the Ordinary

The above story reminds me of the story of Moses being called through the burning bush. While shepherding in the desert of the Sinai one day he sees a bush that is aflame, but is not being consumed. He draws near to see what is going on, and encounters God who calls him to "take off your shoes, for you are standing on Holy Ground!" He does, and God tells him to go to Egypt and lead the Hebrew people from slavery to freedom in the Promised Land.

Someone has said of this account: A few take off their shoes, hear, see, and go, while others stand around and pick blackberries.

After I told this story one Sunday, a woman in the congregation presented me with a pint of blackberries she had picked – not knowing the story I was going to tell! I was speechless, except for an appreciative "thank you!" I did feel a little strange holding the berries in one had, while shaking hands with the other! The very observant parishioner might have noticed that there stood their pastor with his shoes on, and a pint of berries in his hand!

(**Message:** Just as God became ordinary flesh with an ordinary mother, so He comes to us so often in the *ordinary* things – *all about us – every* day!)

*****

201. Amazing Grace
Prior to her death, my greatest fear was that I would line up at the Pearly Gates behind Mother Teresa, and St. Peter would say, "You know, Mother Teresa, you should have done more!"

  (**Message:** The Apostle Paul reminds us that it is: "By grace you have been saved through faith, this is not your own doing, it is a gift from God." Ephesians 2:8)

*****

202. Help – or – Fear
Abraham Lincoln was a man who enjoyed telling humorous stories. One such tale that is accredited to him involves some wild boar hunters. They were out in the woods when several of the vicious beasts came charging out at them from the underbrush. All of the hunters made it up trees except one hunter. The best he could do was to grab one of the animals by the ears. A furious struggle ensued in which the hunter narrowly escaped the boar's razor teeth. But growing tired, he cried out to his companions in the treetops: "Boys, come down here and help me let this thing lose!"

  (**Application:** There are times when we, as my father used to say, "Bite off more than we can chew!" We "take the bull by the horns" only to find ourselves overpowered! Psalm 124:8 declares: "Our help is in the name of the Lord who made heaven and earth.")

*****

203. Holy Communion
In a church's preschool the teacher asked three students to share, after a night to think about it, something that reminded each of his or her faith. She was sensitive in her selection to include one from each of the following faith walks: Roman Catholic, United Methodist, and Jewish.

The following day the teacher started with the three, for she knew they were eager to share what they had brought. The Jewish lad held up a star, and said: "This is the Star of David." The Catholic girl showed the class a cross with Jesus hanging on it, and said: "This is a crucifix." Finally, it was the Methodist boy's turn. He said, "I am a Methodist, and this is a casserole!"

(**Message:** It is appropriate that our remembrance of the Lord centers around a Meal – the Last Supper!)

*****

204. No Fault?
I said in the Introduction that you should avoid Jesus' humor if you want a laugh, second to that are other Biblical passages that are funny, but are not supposed to be! So, let me dare point out some humor elsewhere in the Bible.

As part of the creation story in Genesis 3:9-14, God comes looking for Adam. (It is hard for God to find this slippery critter that He has made!) Adam's reason for hiding was because he was naked! (Who was he hiding from? – Now do not get theological with me here appreciate the humor.)

God realizes that this creature of His has been eating fruit from the forbidden tree! (If you want your children to do something, tell them it is forbidden for them to do!) But, does ole Adam admit his sin, not on your life! After all, he has the woman to blame, and blame her he does. God plays along, and approaches the woman, who by the way has *not* been hiding. God asks her if what He has heard is true. Like a good politician of today, she does not answer the question, but passes the blame off on a snake – how low can you get? Thus, began the custom of buck-passing, and we have all been good at it ever since.

(**Application:** Since none of this is supposed to be funny, we can appreciate the fact that the central message is what we could call the "No Fault Dilemma.")

*****

205. Confusion
In Daniel 3:19-28 we have the story of Shadrach, Meshach, and Abednego in the fiery furnace, or as one child interpreted the names of the

three men: "My shack, your shack, and in the bed he goes."

(**Application:** We can all get tongue-tied on some Biblical name – these are no exception!)

*****

206. Consequences
A colleague in the ministry, Dennis Bowling, tells of serving Holy Communion at his church in Mississippi. A very rambunctious boy, known for his misbehavior, came forward with his mother. He took the elements all right, but suddenly cried out in pain. He had sucked his tongue up inside the small glass, and could not get it loose!

His mother tried to pull the glass off – to no avail. Dennis tried his hand at it: giving a good tug, but the child shrieked in pain. Finally, his grandmother, who had been kneeling next to him all along, slipped her finger down beside his tongue, breaking the vacuum, and setting the youngster free – to commune again!

(**Application:** The mischievous tricks of childhood often have little consequence, but the sins of adulthood can have more dire consequences! See Numbers 32:23b)

*****

207. Embarrassing Blunders
My dear friend, the late Reverend Bill O'Quinn, had a unique way of welcoming visitors to Sunday morning worship. He had his ushers trained to watch for newcomers, get their name, write it down, and right before worship was to begin, come up and hand the names to Bill. Bill could then say, "We welcome to worship today here at Platte Woods Bob and Tammy Thixton… But one Sunday Bill misread the name of a Hispanic couple by the name of Barbados. He said instead: "We welcome the burritos to worship today."

(**Application:** Our slips of the tongue can bring much embarrassment sometimes! – See James 3:5ff)

*****

208. Short Takes on Frustrations:
A woman was telling her neighbor about a new book on weight loss she

had purchased a couple of weeks before. It cost her $20. "How much have you lost?" asked the neighbor. "$20," came the reply.

~~~~~~

A man placed an ad in the Atlanta Constitution: "Big Bertha golf clubs with bag for sale. Putter bent. Asking $800, but will trade for psychotherapy."

~~~~~~

It is said that a mother found on the back of the new stroller she purchased for her infant the following advisory: "Warning! Remove the child before folding up the stroller!"

~~~~~~

A fisherman, who lives in Seattle, accidentally left his day's catch under the seat of the bus. A few days later the newspaper carried this ad: "If the person who left a bucket of fish on the No. 47 bus would care to come to the bus garage, he can have the bus!"

(**Application:** We do some foolish things at times! Thank God for grace, and a chance to learn from our mistakes!)

*****

209. Aging

Some grandparents in the congregation told me how they had taken their three year old grandson to see his great grandfather for the first time. On the way they explained that the gentleman they were going to visit was not just his grandpa, but his *great* grandpa. He seemed eager to meet the elderly man.

When they arrived they had to shout to great grandfather, because he was hard of hearing. He could not see too well, for he asked for his glasses with the thick lenses to see the boy. He struggled to get up, and when he did he staggered as he walked.

On the way home their grandson piped up, and asked: "Meme, what is so *great* about *that* grandpa?"

(**Application:** Leave it to the young to tell it like it is! – See Psalm 8:2)

210. Heaven

Years ago I visited a woman who had just been wheeled back from surgery. She was still pretty groggy. The hospital was right beside the Presbyterian Church. As I came in the room, the chimes in the church carillon were sounding forth in majestic harmony. I heard her murmur, in her half conscious state, "I must be in Heaven!" Then looking up, she saw me coming to her bedside, and added: "No, it can't be, here's Reverend Moore."

(**Application:** Well, I *hope* to join the saints above! Heaven: like a loving father's house, where the Lord has "prepared a place" at His table for you!" See John 14:1ff)

*****

211. Forgiveness

In a drought-stricken section of the country, a farmer went to town to talk with his banker. He told the banker: "Mr. Thatcher, I have good news, and bad news. The bad news: you know that loan I have with you on the farm?" "Yes, Jim," responded the banker hesitantly. "Well, I am not going to be able to pay you anything on the principal or interest this year. And the loan on the new tractor?" "Yes, Jim." "I won't be able to do anything on that either." "The *good* news: I still plan to keep you as my banker!"

(**Application:** God does not come out even that good with us! But the Good News is that God has cancelled our debt! He has nailed it to the Cross! - Colossians 2:13-14

*****

212. Fathers

Two boys were walking home from Sunday School. "Do you believe all that stuff about the devil?" one asked the other. "Naw," came the response. "It is like Santa Claus – it's your *Dad*!"

(**Application:** When they discipline us, we may think our father is the devil at the time, but there will come a time when we thank him for caring! – Proverbs 22:6)

*****

213. Hymns
Some hymns appropriate for us who are getting older:
- o "Just a *Slower* Walk with Thee"
- o "Precious Lord Take My Hand *and Help Me Get Up!*"
- o "Blessed *In*surance!"
- o "Guide Me O Thou Great Jehovah" (Parking lot song!)
- o "I'll Praise My Maker *When* I've Breath"
- o "For the Beauty of the *Girth*"
- o "I Love to Tell the *Stories*"
- o "Ask Ye What Great Thing I *Knew*"
- o "Who Is *That* in Yonder Stall" (Restroom song)
- o "Were You There" (Centennial song)
- o "I Surrender *Some*" (Financial planning song)
- o "And Can It Be that I Should Gain" (Weight watchers song)
- o "*We Should NOT be* Climbing Jacob's Ladder"
- o "*Help* Thou My Vision" – ("Be Thou My Vision")
- o "*Left* It There" – ("Leave It There")
- o "And Are We Yet Alive" – (Song of the Centenarians)

(**Application:** It is fun getting old, and getting funnier all the time! – First three hymn titles above were copied from unknown author)

*****

214. Hospitality
I went to visit my sister, Marilyn in the hospital. There was another patient in the room. As I entered, a nurse, who was also there, recognized me, and said, "Hello, Reverend Moore."

I visited a while, then had prayer with her. As I prepared to leave, I leaned down and gave her a kiss. After I left the room, my sister's roommate said: "Gee, your pastor is a *lot* friendlier than mine!"

(**Application:** Seriously, the author of Hebrews encourages us to show hospitality to strangers, for "thereby some have entertained angels unawares." Hebrews 13:2)

*****

215. Trials
A small Bible publishing company's business fell on hard times. After

doing all they could to keep it afloat, they finally had to file for Chapter 11 verses 1-14.

    (**Application:** I believe it was E. Stanley Jones who said: "Hard knocks come to all of us. We have to decide if they knock us closer to God, or away from Him." – Read Psalm 46)

*****

216. Trials

Sam and Ted were hiking in the mountains when they saw a mountain lion in their path about 50 yards away. Ted slowly took his backpack off, and began retreating back down the trail. Sam said, "Ted, you fool, you don't think you can outrun a mountain lion, do you?" "I don't have to," he said, "All I have to do is to outrun *you*!"

    (**Application:** A friend stands by you in trial! – I Chronicles 12:17)

*****

217. Giving

Jack Benny, who was accused of being extremely tight with his money, had in one of his comedy routines a robber put a gun to his ribs and demand: "Your money or your life!" There was a long pause. The robber repeats his demand. Finally, Jack says, "I'm thinking, I'm thinking!"

    (**Application:** Sometimes persons forget that God expects followers of the Crucified to make a sacrificial gift, *not* because we have a gun to our head, but because we *love* the One who sacrificed all for us: Jesus Christ!" – Read Malachi 3:7b-10.)

*****

218. Counseling Solutions

My father served as a lay pastor for many years. A story is told of one such pastor, who had no higher education, yet who was very successful in helping persons who came to him for counseling. Because of this, his fame spread throughout the county!

Finally, it was brought to the attention of his District Superintendent. The DS called the clergyman in to find out more about what he was doing, and to see why he was so successful.

On the day of his appointment, the pastor sat across the large desk from the Superintendent, who asked: "Tell me the secret to your success in helping persons through your counseling." "Well," began the preacher modestly, "I just ask them questions until I figure out which of the Ten Commandments they have broken, and then I tell them to stop it."

(**Application:** Often the solution to our problems is fairly simple, and the Scriptures offer many solutions!)

*****

219. Commitment

The new recruit had drawn guard duty at the gate to the naval base. He was given strict orders to let no one through who did not show a special pass. His first test came when a chauffer driven admiral's limousine slowed. The guard jumped in front of the car stopping it!

As the guard stepped up to the driver's window, the admiral hollered from the backseat: "Drive on!" "I'm sorry, sir," said the guard apologetically, "I am new at this, but if you drive on, who do I shoot, you or your driver?"

(**Application:** We have to admire one thing in the guard: commitment to task, not what is politically expedient! Scripture teaches us to be committed to the law of Love above all! – See John 15:12-14)

*****

220. Motivating with Love

Back in the early 1900s a Quaker in Pennsylvania had a mule that truly tested his patience! One day the mule balked, and would not move.

The farmer turned loose of the plow, and walked up in front of the beast. With his finger lashing out at the mule, he shouted: "Jenny! Thou knowest that because of my religion, I cannot whip thee, or curse thee. But what thou does not know is, I can sell thee to a Methodist who will beat the stuffin' out of thee!"

(**Application:** In Genesis 1:31 God declares all creation good – even stubborn animals. We are to learn how to rule over them – in love.)

221. Faith: Would you give your Life for it?

The Jesus Seminar has received a lot of press over their controversial attempt to discover the One behind the Gospels, by voting as to what should go, and what should be included in the holy writ. It is said that four members of the group, all professors from liberal seminaries, enjoyed getting together after their sessions for coffee to discuss interpretive issues related to the New Testament.

One day they got into a heated debate which split them three to one. The one felt that the others had unduly ganged up on her, so in the middle of a discussion that had turned to shouting, she simply bowed her head, and said: "Lord! I know I am right, and they are wrong! So, give a sign for all of us to see!"

Immediately lightning flashed, and a thunderous voice boomed: "She is right!" "Did you hear that?" the lone professor declared, feeling vindicated. Then one of the others conceded: "So, that makes it 3 to 2!" – Go figure!

(**Application:** It is said that most all of the apostles gave their lives for their faith. Nothing short of being *convinced* that the Savior died and arose again, would explain the martyrdom of these men! – See I Corinthians 15:12-19, esp. v. 19; also: Proverbs 3:5)

*****

222. Short Takes on Marriage:

The tombstone read: "Elsie Holman Riley, born March 28, 1900 and died January 1, 1970," then beneath it gave this epitaph: "She lived with her husband for 50 years, and died in confident hope of a better life!"

~~~~~

A couple went to a marriage counselor to discuss the problems they were having. The counselor, trying to get in touch with what was going on, asked the woman: "Madam, do you wake up grumpy?" "No, she said, "I let him sleep as long as he wants!"

~~~~~~

One country song states: "I'm so miserable without you, it's almost like having you here!"

~~~~~~

A woman, who had been married four times, was asked by a former classmate at their class reunion: "Why were you married so many times?" She answered: "First, I married a banker. Then I got hitched up with this actor. Then this preacher came along, and I married him. Finally, I married an undertaker." Then she added: "I looked at it this way: One for the money, Two for the show, Three to get ready, and Four to go!"

(**Application:** A sense of humor is critical part of a happy marriage!)

*****

223. Parenting
Mark Twain once gave some advice to parents: "When a child turns thirteen, stick him/her in a barrel, and nail the lid shut. Feed them through the knothole. When he/she turns sixteen – *plug the hole!*"

(**Application:** With all the reported abuse going on, please know that Twain was just *kidding*! Seriously, I am deeply concerned that the average home in America has plenty to eat in the freezer, but not enough *spiritual* food to last through the "night!" Proverbs 22:6)

*****

224. Fears -- Realized
A woman told me that one Saturday she thought her three elementary aged children were watching television, but since they were unusually quiet, she went in to check on them.

There they were in the living room floor playing with three baby skunks! She was horrified, and in the process screamed. That scared the children, who each reacted in the same way: they squeezed the skunks they were holding. – Skunks do not like to be squeezed! – You know the rest of this disaster!

(**Application:** Fears have a way of being realized whether they be in an individual's life, or in the case of a nation! – Proverbs 3:5)

*****

225. Pessimism – or – Fear
Old Virgil ran a gas station and bait shop down in the Boot Heel of Missouri. He did not open until noon. A young entrepreneur came in to his

shop, and suggested that his business would improve if he opened earlier. "I don't think so," drawled the owner, "because I lose money every day as it is. Why, if I stayed open eight hours a day, I'd be broke in a week!"

(**Application:** Pessimism, like fear, realizes itself in negative results!)

*****

226. Our Nation
Someone has said that if Patrick Henry thought taxation without representation was bad, he should see it *with* representation!

(**Application:** Seriously, we should be so grateful to be able to pay taxes in this imperfect, *great* Land!)

*****

227. Justice
Down in the Ozarks an attorney was pleading his first case. A train had struck 24 hogs that had gotten out of the pasture – killing them all! He was suing the Frisco Railroad for damages, on behalf of his client. In his closing, the young attorney wanted to impress on the jury the magnitude of the loss, so as he came to the climax of his argument, he cried, "Twenty-four hogs! Twenty-four hogs, ladies and gentlemen! That's twice as many as are here in this jury box!" – Needless to say, he lost the case!

(**Application:** The jury is out in our case. But God, the great Judge of the Universe, has come down and taken our place as defendant – even to dying, dying on a Cross! – See: I Timothy 1:15)

*****

228. Troubles
Mack was out playing golf with a buddy. He was famous for slicing the ball. On the eighth hole a police officer walked up. He asked Mack, as he pointed toward a dwelling, "Did you hit a ball that sliced over toward that house?" "Yes, I did," admitted Mack. "Well, the ball went through an open window, broke a vase, which scared the family's dog. The dog bounded out of the open window into the street, causing an accident!" "What can I do?" asked Mack repentantly. "Well," said the officer, "You

need to keep your head down and your arm straight!"

(**Application:** The Psalmist writes: "GOD is our refuge and strength, a very present help in trouble." 46:1.)

*****

229. Critics
A rural preacher in North Carolina was asked how large his country church was. He said, "We have 50 members." When asked how many were active, he responded: "All of them. Twenty-five are for me, and twenty-five are against me!"

(**Application:** Most citizens, and probably every public figure, have those who are for them, and those who are against them. The key is to be able to maintain Godly principles in spite of one's critics!)

*****

230. Spiritual Disciplines
Back in the hills of eastern Kentucky there was a revival meetin' – as they called it. As at every revival, Billy Bob would come down the center aisle, and fall on his knees to get converted. There he would raise his arms up to the heavens, and cry: "Fill me, Lord! Fill me!" Within a couple of weeks, he had backslid into his old ways of carousing and stealing.

The people had witnessed this at several of their annual revivals, so when the Fall revival came around again, and Billy Bob came and fell on his knees crying: "Fill me, Lord! Fill me!" Someone in the back shouted: "Don't do it, Lord! He leaks!"

(**Application:** We all leak a little! But God calls us through His Word to honor the disciplines of prayer, worship, giving, and service – to keep us disciplined in the faith, and filled with the Love and Presence of God! – See: Matthew 6:2-21)

*****

231. Trials
In 1985 I took my first plane ride. I must admit I had some reservations about it. After all, they went and had to name the place where you hopefully will land, a "Terminal!" All I had ever connected to such a word,

while pastoring my flock, was someone who was preparing to DIE! "Why couldn't they just call it a depot?" I thought.

But I, along with some other new District Superintendents of the Missouri Area, flew to South Carolina for training. I boarded the plane, and hardly was I seated when this stewardess stood up and began preparing us for a crash! "Your seat cushion also serves as a flotation device!" Thanks, I thought! I would have much preferred if she had said, "Your seat cushion has a parachute in it!" That would sound more practical! Then she told us if the plane sprang a leak, and lost its (our) air, a mask would fall out of the overhead compartment somehow. I had just filled that with my carry-on, and mine did not have an air mask in it! The folks around me did not look like the type who might share theirs either! So, I tried to breathe a little extra to keep myself extra oxygenated just in case!

We took off, and there were all kinds of strange sounds the stewardess didn't tell us about! The bottom sounded like it was breaking up when we were hardly off the tarmac! I thought of going to the exit, but no one else was, so I thought what the heck! Ya gotta go when ya gotta go!

At cruising altitude, the pilot came on and spoke to tell us we were at 30,000 feet and traveling at 500 miles per hour. It was reassuring to finally know that there was a pilot up there who was alert, and knew how fast we were flying.

It was about this time that I got to thinking about the little windows down both sides. *"Why?"* I thought, "Such *little* windows?" I would feel much better, knowing I could get out of one of those things in an emergency, than having to fight with everyone else over the "exit" twelve rows ahead! I figured the 6 foot 300 pound football player-looking fellow behind me would crush me in the aisle – right down there with that strip of lights that are supposed to help if the cabin is full of smoke! – Holy smoke! I tried not to think of *all* the options for dying!

Finally, calmer thinking came to my mind, and I could understand why they did not tell us to exit the window beside us because the lady beside my window was not going to make it anyway. So, I hummed: "Nearer My God to Thee" the rest of the way to Atlanta, in spite of her rude glances! Some people just do not know how to relax!

We *did* land, and as we were cruising across the tarmac at a mere 50 miles per hour, the pilot came on and told us to remain seated with our seat belts fastened until we stopped. Goodness Jehoshaphat!, He told us we could get up, and walk around when we were traveling at 500 m.p.h. at 30,000 feet! But I was so glad to be on the ground, I did not argue the point.

It was then I realized why the Pope always gets out and kisses the ground when his plane lands. But people were looking, so I did not ask to climb down to the tarmac, and do what I felt like doing!

I have flown many times since, but I shall never forget that first flight!
 (**Application:** Jesus did say: "*Low*, I am with you always!" He did not say, "High" I am with you… But I do fly nevertheless, and I love it! – Actually, Jesus said, "Lo, I am with you…" Matthew 28:20b)

*****

232. Possibilities
There is a lot of talk about research in the field of genetics. Recently, a farmer told his story about his son who is a geneticist. In his work he came up with a way of producing a three-legged chicken! His father had even raised some, and sure enough the three-legged feature was passed on to the offspring! You see his son, and his parents love drumsticks. So, this was a wonderful development! When asked how they tasted, he answered: "I don't know, we haven't been able to catch one yet!"
 (**Application:** There are many possibilities wrought by God. Humanity has only scratched the surface! Albert Einstein believed there had to be a God behind the Universe because of its intricate order and possibilities! – I Corinthians 2:9)

*****

233. Results
The ATF office in Atlanta received a phone call. The voice on the other end said, in a low voice, "My neighbor here in Senoia, Georgia, Fred Thompson, is hiding drugs inside sticks of wood beside his house!"

The next day ATF agents descended on the neighbor's house. With axes in hand, they split every piece of wood in his woodpile! Finding nothing, they apologized to Mr. Thompson, and left.

Hardly had they left, when the neighbor called: "Fred, I see I got your wood split for you, now you owe me one! Say, I need my garden plowed! Would you call…"

(**Application:** We sometimes want to bargain with God to get a blessing, but the problem is not God's reluctance, but ours! We so often neglect asking! – Matthew 7:7-12)

*****

234. Death & Beyond
When Calvin Coolidge was Vice President, he was presiding over the Senate one day when a heated debate broke out between two senators. In a rage, one of the senators told the other he could: "Go to Hell!" The offended senator complained to Coolidge concerning the impropriety of such a statement. Coolidge acted like he was looking through the rules governing the senate; finally he said: "I've been looking over the Rule Book, and you *don't* have to go!"

(**Application:** Only those who know the resurrection power of our Lord can laugh death in the face! Philippians 3:8-11)

*****

235. Giving
I am Scotch-Irish, so I can tell one on the Scotsmen who were known to be frugal. No, they were plain "tight!"

A congregation remodeled the sanctuary. They let the pastor add some things that he deemed necessary. One of these included wiring to the pews, so if someone dozed off during the sermon, he could push the button that directed current to their seat in the pew, and they would be shocked awake! It worked well. The pastor was pleased.

In late October the church began their annual Stewardship Campaign. On Pledge Sunday, the pastor had a mischievous idea. As the service came to a close, he called on all who would tithe a tenth of their income to stand. Then, he leaned on the panel of buttons, and those not standing were jolted out of their seats – all except the three Scotsmen, down on the front row, who were electrocuted!

  (**Application:** Scripture declares that "God loves a cheerful giver." – II Corinthians 9:7)

*****

236. Heaven for Animals?

The telephone at the church rang. It was a Mrs. Smith. She had never attended the church, but explained that her cat, Homer, had just died, and she was wondering if the pastor did funerals for animals. The secretary explained that the pastor was out, and suggested that she call the Baptist Church down the block.

That afternoon the woman called back. She said she had contacted three other churches, and none of the pastors did funerals for animals. Since the pastor was now in, she let him talk to the woman. He was prepared to give the same answer she had gotten from the other pastors, but before he could speak, the grieving woman said as an afterthought: "I was going to give the church, whose pastor did the service, a check for $1,000." "Well," said the pastor, "Why didn't you tell me the cat was a Methodist!"

  (**Application:** I have a feeling that the God, who made the birds of the air, and pets at our feet, has a Special place in Heaven for them too! – Read: Matthew 6:26 – Listen for the Lord's compassion for such as these!)

*****

237. Power / Possibilities

A salesman called on a farmer concerning some farm implements. He found the farmer down by the barn. As they stood visiting with one foot up on the fence, the salesman saw the unusually large hog in the pen. The salesman asked how he got him to grow so large. The farmer said, "Six months ago he got into that shed over there, and ate a stick of dynamite I had in a crate. Then, he ran out, and through the barn. On his way he scared my mule, and the mule kicked him in the side! Why there was a terrible explosion that was heard ten miles away! The barn went up, the mule, and a dozen chickens, and we had a mighty sick hog for a few days!"

(**Application:** This story is truly unbelievable! Yet, Paul calls on us to claim the power available to the Christian. In his own words in II Timothy 3:5 he warns against persons "who hold the *form* of religion, but deny the *power* of it!")

*****

238. Thanksgiving

Years ago a country parson was buying a horse. The owner was an Amish man. He called the horse: "Amazing Grace." He explained to the pastor, to get her to go you do not say, "Giddy up," but: "Praise the Lord!" When you want the horse to stop, you simply say, "Amen."

Well this only added to the horse's attractiveness to the preacher. He paid the man, climbed on his newly purchased steed, and headed home in a gallop! Along the way he decided to detour into an open field, so he could really try her out. He shouted, "Praise the Lord!" and the horse bolted out across the countryside! The horse ran so fast that the parson was afraid he would fall off, so he began to say, "Whoa, whoa, whoa!!" But the horse sped on!

Then the clergyman remembered a deep drop off ahead. He could not, for the life of himself, remember what to tell the horse to stop it. Then, finally, the word came! He yelled, "Amen! Amen!!" The horse skidded to the edge of the precipice! Grateful, the parson sighed with relief saying, "Praise the Lord!!"

(**Application:** In spite of this tale of a horse, it is the grateful heart that time-and-again rescues us from the "pit!" – The Psalms are a glorious reminder of this!)

*****

239. Prayer

The Reverend Dr. Robert Arbaugh tells of a man in a church he was serving who had given a sizeable amount of money to the church. The man was not otherwise very supportive of the church, and an infrequent attendee. Nevertheless, Bob was appreciative of the gift, and went by to see the fellow, and thank him personally.

Bob said that after the usual lighthearted conversation, he thanked the man for his generosity to the church. Then he asked if they could have prayer. They bowed together, and Bob offered a prayer. When he finished, he noticed tears on the man's cheeks. The gentleman finally spoke saying: "That was a *damn* good prayer, preacher!"

(**Application:** God sometimes moves the heart even if the response is not all that proper! – Psalm 42:11)

*****

240. Too Much Prayer?

Several years ago, as I was making my rounds at the hospital, I entered the room of one of my parishioners who had not been feeling well, and was undergoing tests to find out the problem. As I prepared to leave I offered to have prayer with her. Her response was one I had never encountered: "No, that won't be necessary," she said, "Sister Mary was in this morning and had prayer."

(**Message:** I thought, with tongue-in-cheek: "Be careful that you do not overdose on prayer!" In Romans 12:12c Paul urges us to "be *constant* in prayer!" Again in I Thessalonians 5:17 he exhorts us to "pray *without ceasing!*" It is one thing that you can have seconds and thirds of, and not gain weight because of it!

*****

241. Race of Life

A friend of mine had a Kansas City Chiefs' bumper sticker on his car. However, a few weeks later, I noticed that the sticker was gone. I asked about it, and he said that he decided to take it off. As soon as he did, he noticed that his car ran and passed better.

(**Application:** The author of Hebrews challenges us to "run with perseverance the race that is set before us" -- It may not be the race you chose, but it is the race that is "set before you" -- AND it is a Christly race: "looking to Jesus, the pioneer" -- He's blazed our trail for us – "and perfecter of the faith" we learn from Him how to bear a cross, how to love enemies, how to care about the poor and sick, and how to persevere to the end! Hebrews 12:1-2)

*****

242. Short Takes on Christmas:

It was Christmas time, and along with her four children under six years of age, she was shopping. After being at it for several hours she could not get a clerk to wait on her in the department store. Finally, she cornered one, and yelled: "Do I get waited on, or do I turn the kids loose?"

~~~~~

Grandfather asked, "Johnny, did you hear Santa come down the chimney last night?" "No," replied Johnny thoughtfully, "but I did hear what he said when he stumped his toe on the couch!"

~~~~~

I was purchasing an item at Bass Pro. As the clerk was putting it in the bag, she said: "I'm sure your grandson will enjoy playing with that!" "Oh, you are right," I said, then added, "Say, maybe I better get another one!"

~~~~~

A four year old was riding with his parents across town. It was the Christmas season, and many houses were decorated for the occasion. Suddenly, he called out from the back seat: "Look! There is a live fertility scene!"

~~~~~

A three year old was helping her parents decorate the Christmas tree. She was mostly unpacking the ornaments, since the tree was so tall. When she came to an ornament of the baby Jesus lying in the manger, she announced: "And here is baby Jesus in His car seat!"

(**Application:** "God so loved the world that He gave..." John 3:16)

*****

243. Humility or Mistakes
The Right Reverend Charles Hall, Episcopal Bishop of New Hampshire, attended a conference in London. Part of the festivities included a service at Westminster Abbey.

His wife, and another bishop's wife from the states, went shopping that afternoon. Realizing that they were running late for the service, they hailed a taxi saying to the driver, "Take us to the cathedral."

Instead of taking them to the Anglican Cathedral, the driver, being Catholic, took them to the Roman Catholic cathedral. Not realizing the mistake, the women rushed into the cathedral, and up to an usher and said, "We are the bishops' wives. Where are we to sit?" (No one knows the response of the usher, but the story made front page of the London Times the next morning!)

(**Application:** The Holy God chose to lie in a feed trough in a barn in Bethlehem, and yet we are proud! – See James 4:10)

*****

244. Humility
The late Molly Ivans tells of being present at the opening session of the Texas legislature when Speaker Gib Lewis thanked his colleagues for re-electing him Speaker of the House. He concluded his remarks with: "I am filled with humidity!"

(**Application:** It may be easier to be filled with humidity than it is to be filled with humility!)

*****

245. Authority
Back around the turn of the last century a Women's Christian Temperance Union speaker was waxing long on the evils of alcohol. A heckler in the crowd yelled: "Madam, don't you know that Jesus turned the water into wine!" Without missing a beat, the speaker responded: "I know that, but I'd thought a lot more of him if he hadn't done it!"

(**Application:** By what authority do we speak and act? – Matthew 28:18)

*****

246. Prayer
Three laymen from different denominations were having breakfast together. As they visited, one of them brought up the question of whether you need to be in a certain position to pray.

The first man said, "When I pray, I kneel. I think that is important to me." A second said, "When I am really in earnest, I lie facedown to pray." About that time a man from an adjoining table, who had been hearing all of this, said, "Fellows, my best praying took place while I was dangling upside down from a power line at forty feet!"

(**Message:** Our Lord did not emphasize the position for prayer, but he did expect His followers to be persons of prayer! He said, not "if" you pray, but "when" you pray… Matthew 6:5)

*****

247. Prayer
When I was District Superintendent of the Kansas City North District, a pastor told me something amusing that had happened in worship. She was in the midst of her pastoral prayer when a loud whistle sounded in the sanctuary. It sounded like someone had whistled, but she could not imagine why!

After the service, an embarrassed mother came up to her and explained that the culprit was her son. He had wanted in the worst way to learn to whistle. All of his attempts had been in vain. Then she added: "When I heard him cut loose with a whistle I was as startled as everyone else. I was ready to ground him for a week. Then he explained, 'Mother, I was praying: Lord, help me learn to whistle. Suddenly, I felt like I could. So, I tried, and it worked!'" Who can punish a boy for receiving an answer to prayer during worship?

(**Message:** Jesus said, "Ask and it will be given you!" Matthew 7:7)

*****

248. Prayer
We were eating in a local restaurant. The waitress brought the meal, and I led us in prayer. When I finished, I heard a youngster at an adjoining table say, "Daddy, what did that man say to his plate?"

(**Message:** I hope that father took that lad home, and taught him how to pray! Is there a lesson as important to teach our children? "And when you pray…" Matthew 6:5)

*****

249. Fear / Resurrection
A fellow was riding in a taxi in St. Louis, when he leaned forward, and

tapped the driver on the shoulder to tell him something. Suddenly, the driver screamed, jerked the wheel, jumped the curb, and crashed into a light pole!

Only then did the passenger learn the cause for such a violent response. The driver had for 20 years driven a hearse for a funeral home....
    (**Application:** Sometimes past experiences have taught us to fear what in fact needs not be feared at all!)

*****

250. Salvation – or – Baptism
The Baptists were having a revival. Joe Hardy was the town bully, who was feared by all. He caroused with the meanest in the county. He was what the folks in town called: "No good!"

Well, someone talked Joe into going to the "revival meetin'" as it was called. Probably told him that he was afraid to go, which was a sure way to get Joe to do something! Well, everyone was watching Joe with one eye, and the preacher with the other. He seemed attentive, and finally even moved. When the invitation was given, and the congregation began to sing "Just As I Am," Joe shocked everyone by first shaking his head like he was wrestling with a bear, then going forward. That night Joe gave his life to the Lord!

The following Sunday afternoon the pastor was baptizing all who had been converted at the revival. Spectators gathered, along with the congregation, to see if what they had heard was true. Some of them had never witnessed a baptism. So, when it came Joe's turn, one of his old buddies heckled from the crowd: "Preacher, you had better anchor that one out over night!" (Let him soak a while!)
    (**Message:** "Amazing grace, how sweet the sound that saved a wretch like me!" – From hymn by: John Newton, a slave trader, who was miraculously converted! – 1779)

*****

251. Mothers
The second grade teacher had just finished the lesson on magnets. She had illustrated a magnetic field by lowering a magnet into a glass that had

some paper clips in it. Then she lifted out a little bundle of paper clips. Later in the morning she gave the class a pop quiz: "What starts with an "M" and picks things up?" Joseph answered: "A mother!"

(**Application:** God gave mothers a sacred role when He chose Mary to be the mother of our Lord! – Luke 1:26ff)

*****

252. Parenting
When asked what the basic food groups are, one young girl answered: "Canned, frozen, and take out!"

(**Application:** The highest calling in life is to be a parent! To be a *mother* is a step above that!)

*****

253. Sacrifice
Rabbi Mordecai Goodman was seated in his synagogue weeping uncontrollably. He had just learned that his son had deserted the ways of his ancestors, and become a Christian.

Suddenly God spoke: "Rabbi, what is troubling you?" "I am so ashamed," confessed Mordecai, "For my son, my only son, has given up his Jewish heritage to become a Christian!" God said, "Yours too?"

(**Message:** "God *so* loved the world that He gave…" By being a follower, we are in the sacrificing business! – What have you sacrificed for Him lately? – See: John 3:16)

*****

254. Details – or – Perfection
Several years ago I went through a series of allergy shots to give me greater resistance to certain allergens. Following getting your shot, the doctor had you wait for 20 minutes to be sure you did not have a severe allergic reaction.

One day, while waiting to get the O.K. to leave, an old timer, from down in the Ozarks, came in for his first visit. He was given a form with several pages of questions to answer. I surmised that it was his daughter with him, for he began to read most of the questions aloud, and then shared the answer that he thought was appropriate to a given question to see if she would concur.

He read: "Dog?" He said, "I'll put yes to that." Then it asked: "What kind?" His daughter offered: "Dachshund." He said, "I'm just going to put 'dog' again." Then it asked: "What *month* are your symptoms most pronounced?" As He wrote his answer, he mouthed: "Sum—mer."
    (**Application:** Sometimes we perfectionists get carried away with precision. We need to relax, and enjoy more! – John 14:27)

*****

255. Critics
During the French Revolution hundreds were beheaded. It is said that one day three men were taken to the gallows to face death. They included a lawyer, a doctor, and an engineer. The lawyer, accompanied by a priest, was the first to be led forward. He knelt down, placing his head where it was to rest. The blade of the guillotine was released, but it stopped halfway down! The priest announced that God had spoken, and the authorities released the man.

The second victim was the doctor. He stepped forward with his priest at his side. When all was ready, the blade was released, and stopped again halfway down! Again the priest announced Divine intervention, and the authorities reluctantly let the man go.

Finally, it was the engineer's turn. He knelt, but then looked up. Jumping to his feet he cried: "I see the problem!"
    (**Application:** Some folks go through life pointing out the problem, but unlike the engineer they fail to come up with the solution. We need more "engineers.")

*****

256. Short Takes on Knowledge

He walked up to the ticket counter. You could tell he had not flown before. He said, "I want a round trip ticket." The ticket agent asked: "Where to?" He said, "Well, back here of course – duh!"

~~~~~

Back in the 1950s there was this craze over Elvis Presley. My cousin asked our grandfather what his favorite rock group was. He said, "Mount Rushmore."

(O,K., enough of that!!)

*****

257. Joy
Sometimes the words of any public speaker do not come out right. It was Christmas Eve at the church. As was the custom, to close the service, everyone would light a candle symbolizing the birth of the Lord. The pastor started by lighting her candle from the Christ Candle, then the flame was passed to the ushers, who took the light to the congregation. As this solemn moment came to a close, the pastor said in a loud voice: "Now that everyone is *lit*, let's sing 'Joy to the World!'"

(**Application:** Our Joy as Christians does not require being "lit." Our Joy is based in the Lord! Philippians 4:4)

*****

258. Mysteries
As a boy, I remember seeing the newsreels of the kamikaze pilots on their suicide missions against our ships. But I never asked myself the obvious question: "Why did they wear helmets?"

(**Application:** Life is filled with mysteries that we never question. For example, how does light pass through a thick pane of glass, but not a thin sheet of metal? – I Corinthians 15:51)

*****

259. Mysteries
A preacher from down in the hills explained the Creation Story this way: "God took a handful of mud, and made the first man. He then hung him on a barbed wire fence to dry. "Preacher!" interrupted one of the girls, "Where did the barbed wire fence come from?" "It is questions like that that are ruining religion," came his curt reply.

(**Message:** There are some mysteries in regard to the Creation Story, but there are far more when we leave God out of the equation!)

260. Persistence in Prayer

Little Clyde knelt for his bedtime prayers. He prayed: "Lord, bless us all, and please make that bully, who lives down the street, quit hitting me!" Then he added: "By the way, I've mentioned this to you before!"

(**Application:** Jesus said, "Ask and you shall receive…" Matthew 7:7 But this English translation does not do His words justice, for there is a continuum here. What our Lord is actually saying is: "Ask, and keep on asking… Seek, and keep on seeking… Knock, and keep on knocking." Why does our Lord require such of us? So that He might keep us close to Him – lest we get lost!)

*****

261. God's Will

One man, wanting to know what the will of the Lord was on a particular issue, placed his Bible on the window ledge. The idea was that God would cause the wind to blow to reveal a certain page, then he would place his finger on a verse on that page, and see what God was saying to him.

All went well. The wind did blow the pages. He placed his finger on a verse and read: "Judas went out and hanged himself." "Wow!" he thought, "This is not what I was looking for!" So, he turned a page, put his finger down and read: "Whatsoever thou doest, do quickly!"

(**Application:** The *first* step in discovering the will of God is to sincerely yearn to DO God's will. God does not perform for us like a magician doing his tricks for the crowd's entertainment and amusement, but God reveals His will only to those who are ready to get down in the ring, and perform His deeds of love and mercy in our time. Then will be fulfilled: "seek and you will find!" – Matthew 7:7)

*****

262. Eternal Life / Heaven

The late Fred Mackey told me the following story as he lay in the hospital's emergency room, having just been told that he had an aneurism that was separating, and he would die at any moment since he did not want surgery. Pulling his oxygen mask to the side, he said: "I have a joke I want to tell you, Bill. – A man died and went to Heaven. It was so beautiful! The birds were singing, and the flowers were blooming everywhere. The weather was perfect! Then he met his wife, who had preceded him in death. 'Martha!' he cried, 'Do you realize that I could have been here a whole lot sooner if you hadn't given me all that oat bran!' " – Fred and I laughed together. A few hours later he went to that Heaven!

(**Message:** It is a beautiful thing when the saints go to be with their God and Savior, Jesus Christ! – Read: Psalm 116:15)

*****

263. Trust in God

One of my favorite stories is of the man who was driving his sports car down a mountain road when he lost control on a curve, and crashed through the guardrail. As his car went hurtling through space he fell out, and managed to grab a scrub pine growing out of the face of the cliff. There he hung five hundred feet from the bottom, and 500 feet from the top. Knowing that he could not hang on for long, he called out to God: "Lord! Can you hear me?" A booming voice from the heavens answered: "Yes, my son, I hear you!" "Lord!" he answered, "Can you help me?" "Yes, my son, I can help you, but you will first have to turn loose of that tree!" After a pause, the man was heard to say, "Is there anyone else out there who can help me?"

(**Message:** One of the most difficult things for us to do in the Christian life is to let go, and let God! Read: Psalm 31:14-16)

*****

264. Perspective

A city slicker was traveling through the mountains of eastern Tennessee. Suddenly, he slammed on the brakes, backed up, and looked again. Sure enough, right there beside the road in a small orchard was a man on a ladder, holding a young goat up over his head! The goat was eating apples from the tree. The man from the city called out: "Sir, what are you doing?" "Feeding my goat," he replied. "But doesn't it take longer to feed him that way?" "Sure, but what's time to a goat?"

(**Message:** It all depends upon your perspective. The one ran around in a hurry. The other was probably relaxing and entertaining himself while feeding his goat! – See Mark 6:31)

265. Giving
An Episcopal priest in Florida published a "Top Ten" list of what could happen if the parishioners' giving did not keep up with the inflationary spiral of the economy. Here is some of his list:
1. To save on electricity the organ will not be used for worship. Instead, the organist will simply hum the first note of a hymn, then all will sing acappella.
2. There will be no more wine for Communion – grape Kool-Aid will be substituted.
3. No longer can persons sit in "their pew." Who says you bought it anyway?
4. There will be no more first class letters sent with your quarterly gifts-to-date report, instead everyone's giving will be posted in the narthex!

(**Message:** I understand that the giving increased substantially shortly after this notice went out!)

*****

266. Thanksgiving
A grandmother shared with me shortly after Thanksgiving one year, that her 4 year old grandson had eaten Thanksgiving dinner with the family. Wanting to know his impression, she asked: "Benjamin, how did you like the turkey?" He answered, "Well, the turkey was all right, but the bread the turkey had eaten, was delicious!"

(**Application:** Joy is based in the thankful heart! – Colossians 2:6-7)

*****

267. Preparation – or – God's Equipping
I grew up on a small farm. We always had a milk cow, and it was my job to milk night and morning by hand. There are a lot of squeezes in the two gallons of milk that I got twice a day! God was preparing me for the ministry, so I could shake all those hands. I tallied it up, and I shook well over one million three hundred thousand hands in my forty years!

At least daily I had to take the pitch fork, and clean the stall where the cow had been. I would throw the dung out on a pile in front of the barn that would later be spread on the garden plot to grow sweet potatoes, corn, green beans, etc. Isn't it amazing what God can do when all He has to work with is lowly dung?

One morning, after milking the cows, I looked out the doorway of the barn, and there atop that pile was the prettiest bluebird I had ever seen, and it was singing!

(**Application:** When life's trials have piled up on us, can we still sing a song of praise to our God? With the uncertainties of the wilderness all around them, the people of Israel joined with Moses in song! Exodus 15:1f)

*****

268. Trials or Patience

A pastor spotted a young lad trying to sell a lawn mower. He needed one, so he stopped to look it over. He told the boy that he was interested, but first wanted to see it run. He pulled-and-pulled on the cord, but to no avail. Finally, the youngster said, "Sir, you usually have to curse it to get it going." "Well, son," explained the minister diplomatically, "I am a pastor, and I cannot do *that*." The lad smiled and said, "Mister, just keep pulling; it will come back to you!"

(**Message:** Life has its trials, many of which try our patience. – Romans 12:11-12)

*****

269. Short Takes on Marriage & the Family:

She was on the witness stand. The attorney said, "Would you please tell the court your name." She said, "Ernestine McDowell." "Mrs. McDowell, what is your marital status?" "Fair," she replied.

~~~~~

Tim went to see his lawyer. "I want to get a divorce," he said. "My wife hasn't spoken a word to me in three months!" The lawyer thought about it for a moment, then said, "I'd think about that for a while, Tim. Wives like that are hard to find!"

~~~~~

Noah Webster, who compiled the first dictionary, would come down for breakfast every morning, and as soon as he spoke a word, his wife would say, "Now what's *that* supposed to mean?"

~~~~~

Fire swept through the farmer's barn, burning it to the ground. His wife called insurance claims office saying, "Our barn burned to the ground last night. Send us a check for $50,000, the amount it was insured for.

The agent on the other end of the line said, "Madam, I'm sorry, but we don't give out money. We will simply replace the barn." "Oh," replied the woman thoughtfully, "Would you cancel the insurance I have on my husband?"

~~~~~

A three year old was there for the birth of his twin sisters. He looked them over, and noted how pink they were. They both began to cry at the same time – keeping both parents busy jostling them, trying to get them to calm down.

Finally, their brother spoke: "Mom, I think we had better start calling folks now, because these are going to be a whole lot harder to get rid of than the kittens!"

~~~~~

Years ago a young man goofed off, and flunked out of college. To try to soften the blow to his parents, he wrote his mother, and asked her to prepare his Dad for the news. By return mail he received the following reply: "Dad prepared. Prepare yourself!"

*****

270. Short Takes from Every Day Life:

I was in line at the customer service department behind a gentleman with a roll of black soaker hose. When it came his turn, he plunked it down on the counter. The clerk said, "Anything the matter with the hose?" He said, "Yes! It leaks!"

~~~~~

My grandfather, James Wilder Moore, was a blacksmith back at the turn of the last century. He was making horseshoes one day, when a man came into his shop. He was hammering a piece of red hot metal into shape. Some other shoes were cooling nearby, and the visitor picked one up, and immediately dropped it! Granddad said, "Kind of hot, wasn't it?"

"No," said the man – keeping his male pride intact – "it just doesn't take me long to look at a horseshoe!"

~~~~~

An eleven year old boy went to his first scout camp. The first night, he was struggling with homesickness, chigger bites, and the incessant hum of mosquitoes, when he looked out of his tent and saw his first fireflies! He had had all he could take! So, he ran to the scoutmaster's tent, and cried: "Mr. Ivey, Mr. Ivey! Now the mosquitoes are coming after me with flashlights!"

On the *third* day it was no less eventful, and the scoutmaster's patience was wearing thin. So, he decided to call the boy's parents. He told them that Jimmy was having a pretty rough time. He added: "He has a lot of chigger bites, some homesickness, and an old shaggy, stray dog has taken up residence in his tent. "What about the smell?" asked his concerned mother. "Don't worry, the dog seems to be getting used to it!"

*****

271. Mysteries

A man came home from work to find his dog out of the fenced in backyard. The dog was lying on the front porch, with the neighbor's pet rabbit lying dead beside it. The man was beside himself! How could he tell his neighbor?

He got the rabbit away from the dog, took it in the house, bathed it, and even blow-dried the hair (the hare?), then he put it back in its pen in the neighbor's backyard, hoping that the neighbor would think it had died of natural causes.

The neighbor came home, and went out in the backyard to check on some vegetables he was growing, and saw the dead rabbit. Shocked, he went straight to the man's house who had the dog. "Jim!" he said in hushed tones, "Something terrible has happened that you will never believe! Our pet rabbit, Hoppy, died. We buried him in the backyard. But today some sick, crazed person has dug him up, and put him back in his cage!"

  (**Application:** It is sometimes best to tell what you know! We know a Risen Savior, and though the mystery of the resurrection blows some folks away, we know that it is the power of God unto salvation! – John 1:12 & Romans 1:16)

272. Eternal Life

Three persons arrived at the Pearly Gate. One was Mother Teresa, another Dr. Christian Barnard, and the last a CEO of a large HMO. St. Peter recognized Mother Teresa right off, and ushered her in. The second was the famous heart surgeon, Dr. Christian Barnard. He told St. Peter of all the lives he saved, and the quality of life that he made available through his work. He too was welcomed in. Finally, the CEO of a large HMO stepped up. He explained how he tried to help make health care available to persons who otherwise would not be able to afford any. Well, St. Peter stroked his beard thoughtfully as he pondered the plight of this candidate; finally he said, "O.K., you can come in – but you can only stay for three days!"

(**Application:** Fortunately God's grace in Christ makes it possible to all who believe in Him to have *eternal* life! – John 3:16)

*****

273. Parenting

Mother's Day was coming, so the preschool teacher brought up to the class about how hard it is to be a parent today. One youngster, who was eager to share his insights, said, "My daddy slaves away day-after-day, so we can eat. Mom works hard fixing our meals, and washing our clothes. You know I am worried!" "What are you worried about Timmy," asked the teacher. "I am worried that they will try to escape!" said Timmy.

(**Message:** Parenting is probably the most difficult and potentially rewarding task you will ever be a part of in life!)

*****

274. The Church

I could not believe my eyes! The small town newspaper headline read: "Twister Blows Away Methodist Church!" Then a subtitle: "Did no real damage to the town!"

(**Message:** We can pray that that will not be said of our church! – Read Ephesians 5:5)

*****

275. Everlasting Life / Aging

An elderly man shared that he no longer took vitamins. He did *not* pay any attention to the sugar, or sodium content of a food. But the one thing that he *did* look for in his food, was how many *preservatives* it had in it!

(**Application:** We all desire long life, as long as it is a good life, but God does us one far better: He gives us *eternal* life through Jesus Christ our Lord! See Luke 18:29-30)

*****

276. Trials

While serving as pastor at Warsaw, Missouri, I soon discovered that the town "watering hole" was the local drugstore. I found I could take the pulse of the community, and find out more there about who was sick or had died than anywhere else.

One day as I was having coffee with the fellows, I overheard an elderly man speaking in a loud voice to the clerk. He wanted her to help him find some things. First, he asked for corn plasters. Next, he wanted a tube of "BenGay" for his aching joints. Then he asked for some Metamucil. Finally, he needed a cane. After gathering all this items together she totaled it up, and he paid her. Then she said, "Have a nice day!"

(**Application:** Sometime it is hard to "have a nice day!" But even then, we can know the Presence and love of God will go with us! – Psalm 23:4)

*****

277. Power of the Gospel

A widower had just gotten a pacemaker. Since he was feeling so much better, he invited a woman, fifteen years his junior, to a dance. She accepted, and soon they were on the dance floor, keeping up with the best. The band increased the tempo on the next number, and the old gentleman kept right up. But, halfway through he collapsed!

Someone asked if they should call an ambulance. "No," said a close friend, "Call the auto club, they can jump-start him!"

(**Application:** Paul says that we can have a form of religion, but not realize the power available through Christ! – See II Timothy 3:5)

*****

278. Possibilities

I believe it was a Herman cartoon that depicted three convicts hanging on a prison cell wall. They were chained together, and if that were not enough, they were chained to the wall in such a way that they could not touch the floor.

When one of them whispers to the other two: "Now here is my plan…"

>(**Application:** Consider the inadequacy of human action – human possibilities! – See Luke 1:37)

*****

279. Mistakes – or - Encouragement

A young pastor was asked to preach one Sunday evening in his home church. He was delighted, and at the same time nervous. He wanted to do a good job, since many people knew him, and his grandfather was going to be there.

But early in the afternoon he noticed a sore throat coming on, and with it some laryngitis. His granddad said, "Son, let me get you a little brandy for your throat. It will ward off that sore throat, as well as help your voice. Take a sip or two now, and the rest along as you preach."

Well, the young man made it through his sermon, and felt pretty good about it! But, he couldn't wait to hear his grandfather's reaction.

Finally, grandpa got him aside, and said, "Son, I said, 'SIP the brandy,' not gulp it! Second, it was the 'Sermon on the Mount' not the 'Sermon on the Amount.' Third, there are only Ten Commandments, *not* fourteen! Finally, David killed Goliath with a sling and a stone, he didn't 'stomp the hell out of him!'"

>(**Message:** We all make mistakes, some of which are more public than others! Read Acts 9:26-27 where Barnabas took Saul, the sinner redeemed by grace, and helped make him into Paul the greatest missionary/evangelist in the history of Christendom!)

*****

280. Short Takes on Misunderstandings

Back in the Appalachian hill country a man decided to buy his wife a "gin-u-wine" skunk coat that a neighbor, quite talented at the trade, had made. His wife expressed heartfelt gratitude for the gift saying, "Honey, how can sich a purty coat come from sich a foul-smelling animal!"

~~~~~

I came across a filling station down in the Ozarks one Mother's day that had a sign out front which read: "Free carnation for mother with gas."

~~~~~

A four year old boy lived in Chicago where, in Lincoln Park, there is a statue of the famous general, Ulysses S. Grant.

One fourth of July, the youngster's parents took him to see the monument. After finding the park, they soon saw the replica depicting Grant riding high on the back of his horse. The mother explained to the lad that that is General Grant!

After a while they prepared to leave the park for home. Turning back toward the statue, the boy said, "Goodbye General Grant, -- and whoever that is on your back!"

(**Application:** Many misunderstand the Power and involvement of the Lord in human history! We wring our hands at what is happening, and fail to see the Hand of the Lord! Deuteronomy 32:27)

*****

281. Secret Service

Some forty years ago, when I was first beginning my ministry, it was common, especially in small town America, for the customers of barbershops to get awfully quiet when the parson came in. They would be enjoying an "off colored" joke, when the "man (for the vast majority were men) of the cloth" would walk in, and everything would get as quiet as death.

So, being a clergyman, I had to get used to this. I would often comment: "That must have been a good one!" But that would be met with embarrassed silence. They were afraid I might call down fire upon their heads, or do something else religious. Oftentimes there were members of the church I served, waiting for their haircut. They would later tell me what was going on – as if I did not know!

(**Application:** Do we prefer to be a member of the Lord's secret service – who "live it" without telling anyone why? I don't think that a certain joke is a great evil, but prejudice and gossip are. First century Christians often gave their lives for being *identified* as one of His! – Mark 8:34)

*****

282. Honesty

Two college roommates at Duke University each had "A"s in chemistry up until the final exam. The weekend before the exam on Monday, they went up to the University of Virginia to see their girlfriends. They got back at 2:00 a.m. on Monday, then proceeded to oversleep, and missed the final!

They went to the professor and apologized. They told him of the trip, but rather than admit to all of the errors of their ways, they said they had a flat tire on the way home, and if that were not enough, when they went to change it, they found the spare flat too! The professor seemed to buy their alibi, and agreed to let them make up the test the following morning.

When they arrived for the make-up test, the professor put them in different rooms. He gave them one question on chemistry that would be worth 10% of their grade. Then he gave them a second question that was worth 90% of their grade. It read: "Which tire on the car went flat?"

(**Message:** Honesty pays. It may not pay today, or tomorrow, or this year, but in the end it pays! – Romans 6:23)

*****

283. Honesty

Sol was Jewish. He was aware of the dietary law against eating pork of any kind. But his friends had told him repeatedly how good it was!

One day he made plans to entertain some fifty non-Jewish clients in an exquisite restaurant. For the occasion, he ordered a roast pig. When it was brought to the massive table where the guests were all seated, he noticed it had an apple in its mouth, and was garnished on all sides with all kinds of vegetables! With the help of the waiter, they all enjoyed the lush, tender meat and vegetables. It was a perfect evening!

But as they were leaving, he saw his rabbi over in the corner with his wife enjoying a meal together. The rabbi waved, but Sol just nodded, paid, and left.

The next morning Sol went straight to the rabbi's office. "Rabbi, I know you witnessed our dinner last night. I wanted to explain to you. I ordered a vegetable tray. How was I to know how it'd be served!"
    (**Application:** See Numbers 32:23b)

*****

284. Temptation
Ollie and Rollie were two bachelors who were quite religious. Every Sunday they could be found on the front row of the church. The church had a balcony, and one Sunday one of the young women got carried away in the spirit, and fell over the balcony rail. On her way down her full, flowing dress caught on a chandelier, leaving her hanging with her dress up over her head!

The pastor, who saw all of this, quickly grabbed the microphone, and declared: "All heads bowed, and eyes closed, while we rescue this young woman who is hung in the light fixture!" Then he added: "If anyone looks, he will be *struck blind*!"

About that time, Ollie leaned over and whispered, "Rollie, I think I'll risk one eye!"
    (**Message:** Curiosity may have killed the cat, and it can at times get us in a heap of trouble! See II Samuel 11:2f)

*****

285. Taking the Cure
Pete and John shared adjoining farms. Often when they were working their fields, they would stop, and come over to the fence and visit.

Pete confided one day that his massive Black Angus bull was not producing any offspring. Something was the matter with him. "So," Pete shared, "I am going to have the veterinarian check him out."

A couple of weeks later, the two were working the adjoining fields again, and stopped for a visit. John said, "Say, Pete, what did the vet find with your bull?" "Well, John," offered Pete, "He ran several tests on him, and prescribed some pills. I give him one a day, and he has been a different animal ever since!" "What did he give him?" asked John. "I don't remember what it is called," said Pete, "but it tastes a lot like chocolate!"

(**Application:** Christ has the cure for the malady of humankind: Death! See Romans 3:23-24)

*****

286. Miracles
A young lad, new to farming, heard his Dad say to his mother, that he was going to use artificial insemination, so their milk cow could conceive a calf. His son was trying to tell a friend at school about it. He said, "You won't believe it, but we have a cow that is going to have a calf – by artificial inspiration!"

(**Application:** Miracles were commonplace in the first century Church. God has not left the miracle business! How often do we fail to see them: in the birth of a calf, etc. See: Acts 8:13)

*****

287. Self Worth
A four year old girl was standing by the window one rainy day, looking out into an approaching thunderstorm. When the storm got near, the lightning was especially severe. Finally, the girl was heard to say, "Mommy! I think God is trying to take a picture of me!"

(**Message:** The Bible Story tells us over-and-over again that God loves us so much that He has our pictures on His mantle! Yes, God *does* want a picture of you! – See Matthew 10:29-31)

*****

288. Knowledge / Truth
Back at the advent of paper shredders, a manager of a company stood

next to one of the new gizmos. His secretary was home sick. So, turning to one of the employees, who was trying to run some copies, he asked: "Do you know how to run this?" The woman came over, and said, "You turn it on here, and put the paper in there." He did as she explained. There was this grinding noise. Then he said, "Now how do you get it to make *three copies*?"

  (**Message:** Sometimes it is not enough to tell someone what we know. Persons need more! They need the truth – come from God! – John 14:6)

*****

289. Value of Life - Or - Fear

Ranchers in Wyoming were having problems with wolves killing sheep. Since it was open season on wolves, some ranchers offered $100 a pelt to encourage hunting them. Two ranch hands, Sam and Ed, were having trouble making ends meet, so they decided to try their hand at hunting.

They headed out into the wide open spaces, and finally set up camp on a ridge. Hardly had they fallen asleep under the stars when a noise woke Ed. He sat up, and by the light of the fire, could see fifty growling wolves surrounding them on all sides! Ed turned to his companion, and cried hoarsely: "Sam! Sam! Wake up! We're rich!"

  (**Message:** They would be rich if only they were not about to lose their lives! – See Matthew 6:19-21)

*****

290. God's Will

Before signing a $17 million contract to play for the Green Bay Packers, defensive end, Reggie White, said he wanted to go home and pray about where God wanted him to play.

When he got home there was a message on his answering machine, which sounded just like the coach for Green Bay, Mike Holmgren, which said: "Reggie! This is God, go play for Green Bay!"

  (**Application:** If only it was that simple to know the will of God. But it requires much prayer, stillness, the counsel and advice of fellow Christians; and sometimes God gives us a sign to show the way. Read Judges 6:36-40)

291. Change – Or - Courage
Have you heard of the attorney who went to the new restaurant? He asked for a change of menu.

    (**Application:** When one old codger was asked about his life in the local congregation he said, "I have seen a lot of changes over the years – and I've been against every one of them!" II Corinthians 5:6-9)

*****

292. Trials
A farmer owned a mule that was sick. Since he used her to plow, and it was springtime, he thought he had better do something. So, he called the veterinarian.

The vet came out, checked over the mule, then gave the farmer a dozen huge pills to give her: one, three times a day. The farmer said, "That all sounds well and good, Doc, but how do you propose getting these pills down her?" The vet smiled, and said, "Get you a length of PVC pipe, just large enough to hold the pill. Put one end down the mule's throat, then blow on the other end. She will swallow it."

A few hours later the farmer staggered into the vet's office looking horribly sick himself! "What's the matter, Sam" asked the doctor. Sam said, "The mule blew first!"

    (**Application:** Life has its trials, and certainly Sam had his! – Romans 8:28)

*****

293. Resurrection
The adult Sunday School Class was delving into death and funerals. The leader asked: "What would you like for the pastor to say about you at your funeral?" One man in the back called out: "I would like for her to say, 'Look! He's moving!'"

    (**Message:** There is within all of humanity a need, a deep desire for eternal life! Paul expresses this in Philippians 3:8-11)

*****

294. Hearing Word
The sergeant had about had it with this new group of recruits! So, finally

he barked: "O.K. you idiots, fall out!" The men fell out except for one. As the sergeant glared at him, he responded apologetically: "Sure were a lot of them, sir!"

(**Application:** Sometimes we think the message for us is actually for someone else. God's Word has a way of regularly stepping on our toes. Woe to us if we don't get the message! – Luke 11:28, 31; 14:35)

*****

295. Authority
A young executive and his wife used to share with young parents their "Ten Commandments for Parenting." But after they had two children of their own, they offered: "Three Suggestions that *Might Work* in Childrearing."

(**Message:** By what authority do you speak? Our ultimate authority I believe is two-fold: God's Word, and Christ-like Love. These are the plumb line we can hold up to all actions and words to see if they are of God! – Read: John 13:35)

*****

296. Advice
Pam Hodgskin tells how her son arrived back in the States after serving with the First Marine Division in Iraq. She was there to meet his bus. As she watched him get off, he started to run toward her, but as an afterthought, pulled out his bayonet from his pack, and dashed toward the quartermaster to return it. Her mothering instinct kicked in when she yelled: "Kevin! Don't run with that knife; you could hurt yourself!"

(**Application:** As parents, relatives, pastors, teachers, and friends we must watch that we do not overdo giving advice, for often it is about as practical as this mother's, or the couple's in the preceding story! – Psalm 39:1a)

*****

297. Honesty / Truth
A sign posted over a half-dozen junk cars in a used car lot read: "Today Only: $899! *These won't last long!*"

(**Message:** The owner was telling more truth than some buyers would be aware of! On the other hand, Godly truth cannot be so subtle – hoping the reader will not get the truth – or have to read the fine print to get to the truth. – James 5:12)

*****

298. Answers to Life
A woman came home from the grocery store, and asked her husband, who was seated in his easy chair, what he had been doing. "Killing flies," he said. "How many did you kill?" "Three males and two females," was his quick response. "Now how did you figure *that* out?" "Well," he said, "Three were on the remote, and two were on the telephone!"

(**Application:** Sometimes persons are pretty ingenuous with their answers! How we answer the deep questions of life is what is of critical importance!)

*****

299. Never Underestimate What God can Do!
Our son, Wesley, who is mentally challenged, amazes us again-and-again with what he comes up with!

One day he came down from his room upstairs to announce that he had killed a *female* cockroach. The obvious question is the one we asked: "Wesley, how do you know it was a female?" He said matter-of-factly, "Because it had a uterus!"

(Go figure!)

*****

300. God's Pursuit of Us – OR: Prevenient Grace
A pastor was making house calls. At one house, he felt someone was home, but got no response, so he got one of his cards and wrote on the back: "Revelation 3:20," then put it in the door. (Revelation 3:20 reads: "Behold I stand at the door, and knock.")

While counting the offering the following Sunday the counters came across a note which read: "For the Pastor." They gave it to him, and inside he found: "Genesis 3:10." Which reads: "I heard the sound of you…

and was afraid because I was naked."

 (**Application:** Consider how far God has come to knock at your door! – Over the changes in our lives, the close brushes with death – knocking, knocking!)

*****

301. Fasting
A quotation reminds me of the subject of my next book: my dog, and the lessons that he teaches me. Now for the quote:
 "Dogs look up to people
 Cats look down on people
 Pigs – treat us as equals!" Author Unknown

 (**Application:** Jesus expected his followers to do three things: pray, give, and fast – Matthew 6:16-17 – It is the last of these three, that is the most neglected!)

*****

302. Possibilities
Kevin was an inventive sort of young man. He took his racer bike, and improved upon it by adding high speed tires, and a unique configuration of a suspension. He could hardly wait to try it out! So, he took it for a run, and got it up to 30 m.p.h. with very little effort, and sensed that the bike was only beginning to do what it was capable of.

So, he asked his buddy if he could tie his bike to the back of his Mustang. The friend had reservations about the idea, but he finally agreed. Kevin explained that if he felt they were going too fast, he would honk the horn he had mounted on his handlebars – a large horn with a bulb, that when he squeezed it, let forth with a loud blast!

So, off they went. When they got up to 35 m.p.h. his friend looked into the rear view mirror to be sure all was okay. At about 50 m.p.h. Kevin realized it was all he could do to keep the bike under control. Suddenly a Corvette pulled alongside and his friend forgot all about Kevin, and took off! At 60 m.p.h. Kevin began to honk wildly when the three passed a sheriff's deputy. The deputy clocked them at 65 m.p.h. in a 50 m.p.h. zone, and gaining speed! So, he radioed in: "You will not believe what

I am witnessing out here on Highway 35, there are two cars racing each other, and this guy on a bicycle honking wanting to pass!

    (**Application:** Things are not always the way they seem. Oftentimes God is working, just out of sight, preparing the way for a new day – a special blessing! – Read: Acts 12:6-17)

*****

303. Prayer / Trial

The Reverend J.D. Prater, the first pastor I remember at our church in Lebanon, told a story that is ascribed to Abraham Lincoln. A farmer, who had never been out of the community where he grew up, decided to walk to the city some 20 miles away. He had traveled about 5 miles when the sky turned black, and a storm began rumbling in.

Finally, the storm was so close that the lightning was striking all around him – lighting up the darkened road in front of him. The thunder was deafening! The wind and pounding rain all but blew him off his feet as he stumbled into a ditch. There he just slumped down on his knees, and began to pray: "Lord, if it is all the same to you, give me a little more light, and a lot less noise!"

    (**Application:** Prayer is such an honest conversation with God. Read again the prayer that is Psalm 139.)

*****

304. Prayer

A pastor decided to purchase a female parakeet for companionship. The bird was one that someone did not want, and had brought it by the pet store to find a new owner. The only problem was the bird would swear from time-to-time.

So, one day while visiting her Catholic colleague, she told him about the problem. He said, "Why don't you bring your female bird by to meet my two male parakeets. For one of my birds can repeat the Lord's Prayer, and the other has learned to hold the rosary beads in its claw and say an extemporaneous prayer. Maybe your bird will learn some new words, and forget its previous life."

The preacher agreed, and the next morning took her bird – cage and all – over to the rectory. The priest welcomed her in. Then showed her where she could place her bird, so she could see and hear the priest's. Suddenly, one of the male birds cocked his head to one side, and looked at the newly arrived bird. Then looking back to his companion he said: "Mike! Put your beads down. Our prayers have been answered!"

(**Application:** The more we pray, the more convinced we become of the fact that many blessings would not come our way if we did not pray! God, in His wisdom, has deemed it necessary for us to ask before we receive certain things. Read: James 5:13-15)

*****

305. Value / Self-Worth
Rabbi Stephen Wise tells of attending a formal dinner in Boston. He was seated next to a gentleman who was from a long line of New England aristocrats. During the conversation that ensued, the gentleman said in a falsely hushed sense: "One of my ancestors signed the Declaration of Independence!" The rabbi smiled and nodded, then said in a similar tone: "One of mine signed the Ten Commandments!"

(**Application:** Our value and self-worth does not come from who our ancestors were, or in how much we have, or… Our worth comes solely from our Maker! Without God we are but worm food! And the inexplicable Good News is spelled out for us in Romans 8:39 in the love of God!)

*****

306. Humble Witness
A very religious, elderly man was unhappy with the world he lived in! He was unhappy with other church members, community leaders, the schools, and the national government – he felt all were "going to Hell in a hand basket!" He often wrote letters to the editor of the paper of his views in which he condemned the sinners – one of which he was not.

One day a reporter from the paper interviewed him. (Yes, it was a really slow day for news!) The reporter asked: "Is it true that you believe that only you and your wife, Mary, are going to Heaven?" He pondered the question for a moment, then answered: "Well, I'm not too sure about Mary."

(**Application:** Self-righteousness wins few converts, and drives many away from the Lord! Contrast such an attitude to that of the greatest missionary/evangelist, Paul, who wrote: Romans 5:8-11.)

*****

307. Practicing Faith
Because our son, William, and I share the same first name, someone asked if *he* was the preacher. William, who is a doctor, replied: "No, it is my father who preaches. – I practice."
(**Application:** Jesus said, "Not everyone who says to me: 'Lord, Lord' will enter the Kingdom, but he who does the will of my Father in Heaven." – Matthew 7:21)

*****

308. Heaven
Riding back from the cemetery with his one surviving grandmother, five year old Jimmy had taken note of what the pastor had said about what a wonderful place Heaven will be. He said, "Is grandpa in Heaven?" She said, "Yes, honey, he is." "How old was he?" "He was 85 years old." "How old are *you*?" "I am 87 years old." "Well," said Jimmy thoughtfully, "I sure hope God hasn't forgotten you!"
(**Application:** "No eye has seen, nor ear heard, nor the heart of man conceived, what God has prepared for those who love Him!" I Corinthians 2:9 – Heaven is far more glorious than all our imaginings, in other words!)

*****

309. Fears
Back in the early 1900s a pastor was visiting persons around his country church. He went up on the front porch of a family he had not met. The door was standing open, and just the screen door separated the inside from the out. As he knocked, he heard a man's voice: "Tommy, get the knife, it's the preacher!" Of course he jumped off the porch and ran to the car! But as, with keys in hand, he was about to get in the man came out onto the porch laughing uncontrollably. He yelled: "Preacher! Don't leave. We have trouble with this screen door sticking. We have to open

it with a knife!"

     (**Message:** Fears often amount to little more than what the pastor faced. We imagine them to be far worse than they turn out to be! – Consider what Moses faced in Exodus 3:1-12)

*****

310. Possibilities – or – Providence
Ralph and Harry were bear hunting in the wilds of Alaska. They had rented a log cabin near a river. The mountains made for a majestic sight!

On their first morning as they were preparing for the hunt, Ralph went down to the stream to get some water to boil for coffee. On his way back, a massive grizzly bear charged out of the underbrush! Ralph ran for his life for the cabin, with the bear gaining on him with each step! When he reached the steps to the cabin, he fell, and the bear went sailing over him, crashing through the front door. With that, Ralph got up, and called out: "Harry! You skin that one, I will go get another!"

     (**Message:** I believe it is a line from an old country gospel song that goes: "Lawd! If you don't help me, don't help that bear!")

*****

311. Communion
The parson told his family that he was going to give blood, and then visit the folks who were in the hospitals before returning for lunch.

After her Daddy had gone, four year old Sarah said, "Mommy, where is Daddy going?" Her mother explained: "Your father is going to give blood." The four year old pondered that for a while, then finally said, "But we know it's really grape juice, don't we."

     (**Message:** The bread and – for most of us Protestants – the juice are a means through which the Risen Christ's real Presence is made known! – Matthew 26:26-29)

*****

312. Short Takes on Parenting / Influence:

It is not easy raising children! In order for a child to become clean, something else must become dirty.

After a youth outing to the lake with the church group, an irate mother called saying: "Someone must have *stolen* my daughter's bath towel!" "Can you describe it?" asked the Youth Director, hoping to defuse the explosive situation. "Yes, I can. It is white, and has 'Holiday Inn' embossed upon it."

~~~~~

A grandfather was introducing his family when he came to his great grandson. He said, "He is the third degeneration of our family."

~~~~~

The longer it takes to prepare a meal, the less your child will like it!

~~~~~

The Sunday School Class had been learning the Ten Commandments. The teacher asked: "What commandment teaches how to treat our brothers and sisters?" Benjamin raised his hand: "Thou shall not kill," he answered.

(**Message:** "Train up a child in the way he/she should go, and when he/she is old they will not stray from it." Proverbs 22:6)

*****

313. Speaking / Preaching
The pastor was ill. His wife, instead of picking up the thermometer, picked up a barometer. When she checked a few minutes later, it read: "Dry and windy!"

(**Message:** Whatever the Lord lays on our hearts to do, we should give it our all! – Mark 8:34)

*****

314. Nature of God
A group of Roman Catholic Cardinals were discussing the nature of God. Of course they agreed that God was to be addressed as "Father," and surprisingly they felt that when Christ comes again, He would probably come to Rome. Suddenly, they got word that the Pope wanted to see them immediately, so they rushed to his quarters.

The Pope was very solemn when they entered but they could not imagine what news could be so grave. Finally, the holy Father spoke: "God has returned to earth. SHE just called from Salt Lake City!"

(**Message:** Protestants as well as Catholics have a long-standing tradition which views God as masculine in nature. Yet, Jesus said our Lord is like a mother hen – Luke 13:34. God is neither male or female, though "He" can be *like* either depending on His actions.)

*****

315. Short Takes on Marriage:

Have you heard the immortal words of Eve as she stood in the Garden of Eden? She said: "I am the one who wears the *plants* in this family!"

(**Message:** No comment!)

Eve had it made, because at least she did not have to listen to how Adam's mother used to cook!

~~~~~

A widow called the monument company to explain what she wanted on her husband's tombstone: "Rest in Peace – Until We Meet Again!"

~~~~~

Back in the days when the discussion of sex was just beginning to be a subject persons in proper company could speak about, a pastor was asked to speak on the subject at the meeting of the Rotary Club. Because he was a little squeamish about telling his wife, he explained he was going to be talking about yachting.

A few days later his wife ran on to a fellow Rotarian at the grocery store. He commented on what a fine job her husband had done at their meeting.

She gave forth with a skeptical huff, then said: "I can't believe that he would speak on that subject, since he knows so little about it. Once when he tried it, he got sick, and the other time his hat blew off, and he never did find it!"

~~~~~

At a wedding where a couple insisted on changing the vows from "until death do we part" to "as long as love lasts" the pastor in charge gave them paper plates as a wedding gift. He figured they would last longer than their marriage would.

~~~~~

Have you ever noticed when you go to a wedding, before the bride and groom can say, "I will," the ushers are asking whose side are you on!

*****

316. Providence - or - Help from God

A woman locked herself out of her car in a rough section of the city. She did not have a cell phone, and did not know what she would do when she spotted a cleaner's. She went in and asked if she could use a hanger to try and open her car. They accommodated her. She went back out to her car, and was working away when a man came up and said, "Can I help you?" She was reluctant since the man looked like a rough character, but realizing that she was not going to be able to get the door open, she agreed. In thirty seconds he had the door open!

She thanked him profusely, then said, "You must be a Christian!" "No," he said, "I am not. I just yesterday got out of prison for car theft." "Well, praise the Lord!" she cried, "God sent me a professional!"

(**Application:** How often does God send us help in the most unexpected ways! – Read: Hebrews 13:2)

*****

317. Mistakes

Dora Wilson of England saw two men carrying some expensive Persian rugs out of her neighbor's house. Knowing that her neighbors were on vacation, she called out: "What are you doing?" One of the men yelled back: "We are taking the rugs to be cleaned." With that Mrs. Wilson asked: "Will you take mine too?" They did!

(**Application:** We have all made some serious mistakes we wish we could take back. But good can come out of those too – if we learn from them, or if they help us see that things are not what is of most value in life! – Romans 8:28 & Philippians 3:8)

*****

318. No-Fault Dilemma

This man was having some health problems. He was driven nearly to distraction with ringing in his ears, bulging of his eyes, and dizzy spells.

He went to his doctor who had him take a lot of tests, but they led to no diagnosis. He even got a second opinion from a specialist, but still no answers.

Depressed by it all, he decided to get his affairs in order. He made out a will, bought a cemetery plot, and made arrangements with a funeral director.

He also, thought: "If I am going to die in the near future, I am going to live-it-up while I can!" So, he went out and bought a new suit, a shirt, and tie. The clerk looked at the shirt he had picked out, and said: "You got a size 15/34 in that shirt, let me measure you." So, the clerk measured his neck, and said, "You need a size 16." But the man protested: "There is no way I could wear a shirt that big, why just four months ago I bought a size 15 neck in a shirt, and it fit neat and crisp!" The clerk said, "Well, you can go ahead with the 15, but I'll warn you, it will make your ears ring, your eyes bulge, and cause dizzy spells!"

(**Message:** Many of the trials we experience in life, we bring upon ourselves! – Read Romans 5:12-14)

*****

319. Parenting
A mother, along with her nine children, all under eleven years of age, was flying to Germany to join her husband, a colonel in the army, who had been recently assigned there. When she arrived, the German customs agent asked her the usual questions, among them: "Do you have any weapons…" She replied: "If I had any weapons, I would have used them by now!"

(**Application:** God said: "When Israel was a child, I loved him…" Hosea 11:1)

*****

320. Parenting
A stay-at-home Mom reported on the day's activities to her husband as he arrived home from work: "Jimmy cut his first tooth. He took his first step. He fell and knocked out the first tooth, then he said his first word!

*****

321. Discipline
A former Viet Nam Ranger took a job teaching in an inner city school. The principal warned him that the particular class that he had was impossible to keep under control!

On his first day of class, he greeted the students, then opened a window to let in some fresh air. When a breeze blew his tie back over his shoulder, he walked over to his desk, took out a stapler, and proceeded to staple his tie to his breast bone! – The class was well behaved from the day forward!
    (**Message:** "The Lord disciplines those He loves." Hebrews 12:6 – This is no less true of parents and teachers.)

*****

322. Motivation
Several years ago, when Bear Bryant was coach at Texas A & M, the Aggies were the number one team in the nation. In a crucial game, they were playing Arkansas State. In the last quarter Texas was ahead by only one point: 7 to 6.

Quarterback Roddie Osborn was leading his team down the field to what would probably be a sure victory when he made a mistake. Instead of handing it off to his Heisman Trophy winning back to run it on in, Osborn instead passed, and it was intercepted! The back who intercepted it was the fastest man on the field, and Osborn was known for being slow on his feet.

A foot race ensued with Osborn pursuing his opponent down the field, and miraculously tackling him on the 7 yard line! The Aggies defense then held the Razorbacks, and won the game.

After the game, a reporter asked Osborn how on earth did he catch that speedster, and save the game. Glancing over at Coach Bryant, he said, "My opponent was running for a touchdown. I was running for my *life!*"
    (**Message:** When God calls, women and men of faith can do miraculous things, for that is the Biblical promise! Philippians 4:13)

323. Meeting and Greeting

A country church acquired a new pastor. He set out to get acquainted with everyone within ten miles of the church to see if they had a church home, and if not, to invite them to join his congregation.

One family lived at the top of a hill on a gravel road. Not finding them at home, he started back down the hill, but forgot how sharp the curve was at the bottom. As he slid around the corner, he narrowly missed hitting a car coming the other way. The woman in the other car was still shaken when she arrived home to find a calling card on the door which read: "Sorry I missed you. I'll try again later."

(**Application:** It is the duty of every member of Christ's Church to meet and greet strangers in their midst. -- Hebrews 13:12 & I Peter 4:9)

*****

324. Appearances

She was busily preparing supper. In order to fix one dish she needed two tablespoons of catsup. Well, of course, the bottle was practically empty. So, there she was pounding on the bottom of the bottle trying to get the rest of that second tablespoon, when the doorbell rang. She called out to her five year old, "Honey! See who is at the door!" The youngster went to the door, and there stood the pastor of the church. He looked down at the little girl, and said, "Where is your mother?" "Oh," said the child, "She is out in the kitchen hitting the bottle!"

*****

325. Parenting

A third grader had an assignment to write a 150 word essay on something they did over the weekend. Sean wrote, "Dad bought a new car, and we went for a drive down to the lake. When we started back, the car quit, and would not go! (I know this is only 26 words, but you wouldn't want to hear the rest!)

(**Message:** Our tongues can bring blessing or curses. Which is the case with your tongue? – James 3:6-10)

*****

326. Rejoice

The Reverend Dennis Bowling, had the devotion for Staff Meeting one week. He held up a picture of DaVinci's "Last Supper," then said, "Do you know what Jesus said to the disciples right before the event this picture portrays? He said, 'O.K. fellows, everyone on this side of the Table for a picture.'"

    (**Application:** Dennis shared that he told that in a sermon one Sunday at a church in Mississippi. Afterward one of the old saints of the congregation, gave him a tongue-lashing for his sacrilege. I think Jesus would have laughed – at the joke!)

*****

327. Christmas / Gifts

A woman took advantage of the after Christmas sale one year by buying several boxes of discounted Christmas cards. She really got a bargain – or so she thought. On the outside was "Merry Christmas!" with a tree, underneath which was a pile of colorful packages.

With Thanksgiving past, she quickly signed the cards and sent them to about one hundred friends and relatives. Only then did she take time to pick up the one remaining card, and read the little jingle inside. It read: "This card is just to say a little gift is on the way!"

    (**Application:** "God SO loved that He gave" – not accidentally, or unintentionally but from the heart a very expensive, costly Gift – Himself in the Christ of the Cross! – John 3:16)

*****

328. Remembrance

Former Evening News anchor, Tom Brokaw tells of being in Bloomingdale's in New York when he noticed a man staring at him. Finally, the man approached, and said, "I know who you are! You're Tom Brokaw! You used to do the news for us in Omaha." Then he added: "Whatever became of you?"

    (**Message:** How soon people forget, or do not notice – but hopefully they will remember "Christ in us." Paul wrote: "For to me to live is Christ, and to die is gain." – Philippians 1:21)

329. Sin & Grace
A pastor took Holy Communion to one of her homebound members. After the small talk, she offered the Holy Sacrament. The woman expressed deep gratitude for the opportunity.

Then her pastor turned to the Communion Service, and began praying the prayer of confession: "O Lord, I have strayed from thy way like a lost sheep. I have followed too much the devices and desires of my own heart. I have grievously sinned against thee in thought and deed…" When she said, "Amen," the elderly woman patted her on the knee, and said, "Pastor, don't worry, I'm sure God will forgive you."
    (**Message:** Too often when we speak of sin, we think of "them," rather than US! – Romans 3:23 & 5:8)

*****

330. Baptism
Back east the Fire Marshall was making the rounds of the churches in a town, checking for safety. As he went down his inspection list with the pastor, he came to question #15: "Do you have a sprinkler system?" The pastor laughed, and said, "You kidding? Why we're Baptists!"
    (**Application:** It is said of us Methodists that we will baptize you by sprinkling, pouring, or immersion – that is true, but someone added: "Or by dry cleaning!"

*****

331. Baptism
It was the Sunday that we were going to baptize our confirmands. It so happened that the week before, the choir had gotten the shipment of new choir robes. So all was lining up to be a very special day!

On Friday afternoon, the custodian discovered that the heater for the baptistry was not working, and now it was too late to get a repairman to fix the problem, so he would just fill it with water, and hope that the water would not be too cold on the January morning of the baptisms 45 hours later.

When the special Sunday came, my wife, Ginya, who is an ordained pastor also, was teaching her Inquirers Class that morning. The subject just worked out to be on baptism, so she told her group that during the following hour they could witness how we baptize persons. For one youth wanted to be baptized by pouring – a rarity in the United Methodist Church – a few wanted to be baptized by sprinkling, and about a dozen would be baptized by immersion in the baptistry.

As the choir gathered in the choir room to put their new robes on, the choir director called them together and announced: "Be careful when you go into the choir loft, for the baptistry is open." (Usually plywood sections covered it when not in use.) The problem was, one of the choir members was in the restroom, and did not get the word!

The choir lined up in the narthex along with the thirty confirmands and clergy. The organist pulled out all the stops as he began the processional hymn. All filed in. The choir, carrying their music folders, opened to the hymn. As we pastors filed into the chancel area, and turned to face the congregation, suddenly there was a great splash! Water came cascading out across the altar. I turned to look down into the baptistry, and there was one of our choir members – totally immersed! Suddenly, one of the men jumped in to rescue her, creating another splash! Finally, both came up out of the floor with water pouring off of them!

Ginya later explained to the Inquirers Class that that is *not* a fourth way we baptize persons!

Our choir member was unhurt, and a great sport, for she thought it was as funny as anyone else did!
    (**Application:** It is not the water that saves us, but the One who Himself submitted to baptism, Jesus Christ our Lord! – Matthew 3:13ff)

*****

332. Baptism
It happened at a First Baptist Church in a small town years ago. The pastor was a retired military officer. For over 20 years he had been used to giving orders, and seeing them carried out without question. Now as pastor of a church, the "troops" were not as obedient. They had their own ideas of how things should be done! As a result there was conflict.

A member had volunteered his time to build new wooden steps down into the baptistry. He had done a good job, but he overlooked one detail: bolting the new steps down.

Sunday came, and a man came forward at the invitation, and gave his life to the Lord. Then as the congregation sang, the pastor retreated to the room off the chancel area to don his chest waders for the baptism. He soon returned, and with the convert in tow, stepped onto the new stairway, which began to float away! Before he could realize what was going on, he found himself falling backward into the water with a mighty splash! In the process he filled his boots to the top! As he struggled to right himself, a choir member said to a staff member nearby: "Should we help?" The staff member mumbled something about letting the ole boy get out himself! After more splashing and gurgling, finally the pastor was able to right himself, but it took two ushers to help lift him out of the water!

   (**Application:** I say it with "tongue in cheek," but these two stories may partly explain why our Lord never baptized anyone, and why the apostle Paul was rather unsure who he had baptized: – very few nevertheless! – I Corinthians 1:14-17)

*****

333. Overwhelming Power
The Sunday School lesson was about putting new wine in old wineskins. The teacher then paused and asked her 5th graders: "What does this mean?" Josh raised his hand, and when called upon said, "It means that if you put new religion in an old man – he will bust!"

   (**Application:** Too often we live (and worry) as though we did not realize that God has the Power to change individuals and nation states! "For such an *overwhelming* Power belongs to God, and *not* to us!" – II Corinthians 4:7b – Jerusalem Bible)

*****

334. Possibilities
During a late evening jog, a man took a shortcut through the cemetery. In the darkness he failed to see a freshly dug grave, and fell in! He tried every conceivable way to get out, but to no avail. Finally, he just sat down

in the corner to wait for morning.

A few minutes later another jogger, taking the shortcut through the cemetery, fell in the grave! The first jogger said, "You can't get out of here!" – But he DID!

(**Application:** When the adrenalin is pumping we can do some amazing things. But nothing compared to when we are doing God's bidding! -- I Samuel 17: 41-17)

*****

335. God Provides

Abraham bought a new computer. He was showing it to his son, Isaac, who said: "Dad, your computer is nice, but it does not have enough memory!" "Don't worry, my son," said Abraham, "God will provide the RAM!"

(**Application:** See Genesis 22:1-14, esp. verse 8a)

*****

336. Self-Discipline

When I was a lad of about 8 years of age, one day Dad brought home a bottle of "Had-a-Call." "Had-a-Call" had been advertised to have many health benefits, not the least of which was a general sense of well being! Now you must realize that my parents were strong teetotalers! But father had heard of the health benefits of this potion, so he bought some at the drugstore to try. He gave each of us the recommended tablespoonful, and we almost immediately felt better! Later Dad read the ingredients, and was shocked to see listed: "75% alcohol."

(**Application:** Scripture tells us that Jesus turned the water into wine. Many good things can be abused, and misused,! Thus, we are called to discipline our lives accordingly. A horse that is not "broken" is of no service. Thus, we must be broken – i.e. get our hands on the reins of our lives lest we become slaves of our passions! — I Corinthians 9:27)

*****

337. Truth – or – Authority

An engineer, a psychologist, and a pastor were hunting in the northern woods of Canada when a snow storm overtook them, and they retreated to a nearby cabin. Finding no one inside, they made themselves at home. There was one unusual thing about the cabin; the heating stove was suspended in the air by wires. Thus, they began to speculate why this was done.

The psychologist said, "It is obvious. The lonely mountain man, isolated from the human contact, must have raised the stove so that he could curl up underneath in a primordial need to seek refuge beneath his mother.

"Nonsense!" cried the engineer, "Anyone can see that the mountain man must have known something about thermodynamics. He elevated the stove so it could disperse the heat more evenly throughout the cabin!"

"With all due respect," countered the preacher, "I'm sure that hanging the stove from the ceiling had spiritual significance. Fire lifted up, has been a religious symbol for eons of time!

About that time there was a noise at the door. It was the trapper who owned the cabin. He welcomed his guests in from the storm, then asked why they were examining his stove with such puzzled looks on their faces?

The pastor explained that they were trying to figure out the meaning of such an arrangement. The trapper said, "I had plenty of wire, but not much stovepipe!"
 (**Application:** And the Jesus Seminar voted on the meaning behind this arrangement, and the three experts missed the truth all together! – Far too often what is obvious is the last thing we think of in our search for truth! – John 8:32)

*****

338. Resurrection
Years ago in the classified ads of the Chicago Times was listed the following: "Tombstone for Sale! Real bargain for someone by the name of Dingo!"

Wouldn't you like to know what happened to the first Dingo? Why didn't

he/she need the tombstone anymore?
(**Application:** Our Lord is the only one I know of who did not need a tombstone! – Mark 16:6)

*****

339. Hearing the Word
A doctor, a lawyer, and a preacher went deer hunting. As they walked into the woods, they all three saw this large buck, and shot simultaneously. The buck dropped to the ground. Then the debate began as to whose shot it was that bagged the trophy.

About that time a Conservation Agent came upon the three. He asked what all the commotion was about. They explained, so he agreed to try and determine which of the three had killed the deer.

He rolled the animal over, and after a short analysis said, "It is quite simple who killed the buck. It was the preacher!" The other two protested, so he explained: "The bullet went in one ear and out the other!"
(**Application:** It has been said that many hearers of the Word, say: "That applies to the person behind me," and so with that person, until the message is passed right out the door! – Matthew 13:13-17)

*****

340. God's Call
A homiletics professor used the great Demosthenes' system, for learning proper enunciation. Demosthenes overcame a speech impediment by putting pebbles in his mouth, and speaking to the sea.

The homiletics professor substituted marbles for the stones. Thus, each student had to practice saying words with a mouth full of marbles. As they progressed, the number of marbles was reduced. He then pronounced them ready to preach – when they had lost all of their marbles!
(**Application:** The central qualification for pastoral ministry is a clear call of God! Without that, all the candidates' talents and abilities will be to no avail! – Read of Isaiah's call in Isaiah 6:1-8)

*****

341. Misunderstanding
Back in the days of prohibition Roman Catholics saw nothing wrong with drinking of alcoholic beverages, but did have a problem with breaking the law. One young associate priest had a member confess that he had made a gallon of whiskey.

The young priest did not know what would be an appropriate penance for such an act, so he called out to the older priest: "Father John! I have a bootlegger, what shall I give him?" The older priest responded: "Why, don't give him any more than two dollars a gallon!"
    (**Application:** What can we give unto God to make our sins right? Nothing, but Christ's sacrifice in our place! – Romans 5:6-11)

*****

342. All Sinners – or – Choir
In the Little Brown Church, the choir director referred to her choir as the "Prison Ensemble." Someone asked why, so she explained: "They are always behind several bars, and often looking for the key."
    (**Application:** Apply it if you dare! – Romans 3:23)

*****

343. Honesty
Charlie and Bill worked together repairing the rain troughs on widow Brown's home. At one point Charlie's language sizzled! The widow overheard the tirade, and called the fellows' boss to complain. He proceeded to call them in to give them a good scolding, and to ask them to explain, for it looked bad for the company!

Bill said, "It is this way, boss. I heat the lead on the ground, then hoist it up to Charlie, who then pours it on the gutter seams. Well, on the day in question, Charlie got careless and spilled some of the hot lead down my neck. So, I said, 'Goodness gracious, Charley, please be more careful!'"
    (**Application:** Dishonesty sometimes seems to pay. Though Bill's understatement was sure to not fool the boss! – Ephesians 4:25-27)

*****

344. Marriage / Love

She called to report a missing person. The 911 operator asked her to explain, so she said, "My husband is missing. He is short, overweight, bald, has a high squeaky voice, bowed legs, and about five days growth of beard." Then she added: "If it is just the same to you, forget that I called!"

(**Application:** How conditional is our love? – I Corinthians 13:8a)

*****

345. Patriotism

Martha Connelly was frequently visited by the Jehovah's Witnesses. She was happy with her Baptist faith, and was becoming more-and-more annoyed by the well-meaning Witnesses. A friend offered a solution: "Buy a flag, and display it on your porch. When they come calling say, 'I will listen to your spiel, only after you join me in the pledge of allegiance.' They will refuse, and that will end the conversation."

Martha was getting desperate, so she decided to give it a try. Two days later, she spotted a woman coming up the walk toward her door with her paraphernalia under her arm. The doorbell rang, and Martha, remembering her friend's advice, opened the door, and said, "I will only listen to what you have to say if you will join me in the pledge of allegiance." Amazingly, her visitor obliged! Then she spoke: "This is the first time in twenty-two years I have been asked to pledge allegiance before trying to sell some Avon!"

(**Application:** Commitment to country is one of the responsibilities of every Christian. – Romans 13:6)

*****

346. Christmas Giving

Several years ago at Christmas time we received a gift from a church member. The attached card read: "Dear Bill, knowing that you do not need the sweets, I am enclosing the candy to Ginya, and nuts to you!"

(**Application:** Since the first Christmas when "God so loved… that He gave…" (John 3:16), Christmas has been a time of giving.

347. Embarrassment
The visiting preacher, John McClure began his week of services at a local church by attending the Kiwanis Club luncheon where he was to be the guest speaker. After lunch he was introduced, and prepared to speak. First, he noted that he had met a reporter from the local paper who was in the audience, so he asked him not to print any funny stories that he told, because he would likely use them at the church throughout the week. The reporter agreed.

However, the guest minister was horrified when in the next day's paper he read: "The guest speaker, Reverend John McClure, told a number of humorous stories that cannot be printed here!"
    (**Application:** Try as we do, sometimes things do not come out the way we wanted! – Romans 7:21-25)

*****

348. Witness – or – Influence
Grandpa was out with his grandson when they drove by the local Burlesque Theater. Gesturing toward the theater, he said, "Son, you should never go in a place like that. You might see something you shouldn't." His grandson nodded in recognition of having received the old sage's advice.

Well, you knowing human nature, know that the first chance he got, the youngster slipped into the theater – to "see what he shouldn't see!" Sure enough, he saw – his grandpa!
    (**Application:** We witness best with our example! Words come cheap, as our Lord says in Matthew 7:21.)

*****

349. Limitations – or – Frustrations
Tim, being the youngest, was the last of his siblings to go off to college. He had learned a lot from his older brothers and sisters about the university life. One thing that he knew would be helpful to him was to make a brick bookcase like his oldest brother had made. Since he was graduating, he passed on the boards and bricks to Tim.

A brick bookcase consists of two stacks of bricks – four bricks in each stack, then a board is laid across them. Then two more stacks of bricks. Then another board on top, followed by more.

Tim took the bricks and boards to school with him, placing them in his second story apartment along with his other belongings. He then built his bookcase, and used it all his first year. It was great!

When the school year ended, Tim thought about the bricks, and developed a plan to get them down to his car in a more expeditious fashion. He went to a local Farm & Home store, and purchased a ten gallon, heavy duty plastic bucket, a pulley, and 50 feet of rope. He went up to his apartment, and anchored the pulley outside the window. Then he ran the rope through the pulley leaving equal lengths resting on the ground below. Next, he went down stairs, tied the rope to the bucket, drove a large stake in the ground, and then hoisted the empty bucket up to the window above. Finally, he tied the rope in a bow knot to the stake. Then, climbed the stairs up to his apartment, thinking all the while of how inventive he was!

He entered his apartment, got the bricks, and placed them in the bucket outside the window, being careful to get all he could in it. Then, he went down the stairs, and out on the lawn. He got a firm grip on the rope. Then, with his other hand he untied the rope from the stake in the ground. Suddenly, he was jerked skyward! On the way up he collided with the brick-filled bucket on its way down!

Well, when the bucket hit the ground, it hit with such an impact that the bottom broke out, which released the load of bricks! Yes, he plummeted toward the ground, as the broken bucket collided with him on its way back to the pulley above! This time Tim hit the ground so hard that he was stunned enough that he let go of the rope, and the bucket came back down striking him on the head!
　　　(**Application:** Our best plans can get us in trouble. Thus, we must hold fast to God's Plan spelled out in His Word for each of us! Luke 8:15)

****

Index

The following themes are not necessarily the same as the headings given to the stories in this book.

Anger	#48, 87
Authority	#221, 245, 295, 337
Awe / Reverence	#131, 200
Baptism	#76, 79, 113, 330, 331, 332
Call / Guidance	#115, 163, 195, 196, 261, 290, 339, 340, 341
Children	#54, 205
Choir	#342
Christmas	#194, 242, 257, 327, 346
Church / Ecumenism / Hospitality	#115, 122, 124, 141, 154, 155, 156, 166, 169, 203, 207, 213, 214, 274, 323
Commitment / Hypocrisy / Obedience	#16, 30, 38, 90, 116, 120, 171, 172, 219, 220, 253, 281, 306
Communion	#207, 311
Consequences / Judgment	#10, 22, 53, 69, 94, 98, 138, 182, 187, 190, 201, 202, 204, 206, 227, 228
Courage / Fear	#11, 50, 52, 55, 56, 71, 91, 108, 149, 179, 180, 194, 224, 225, 231, 308
Critics / Negativism:	63, 104, 130, 198, 199, 229, 255, 291, 306
Death: See "Heaven / Eternal Life"	
Discipline: Children / Us	64, 70, 72, 150, 167, 168, 181, 321, 336
Encouragement	#279
Faith: See "Surrender"	
Fasting	#301
Fear: See "Courage / Fear"	
Giving	#18, 19, 99, 152, 153, 161, 217, 235, 265
God, Nature of	#314
Gossip	#63
Grace / Forgiving Others	#34, 92, 101, 132, 176, 181, 186, 188, 189, 201, 211, 329
Guidance: See "Call"	
Guilt	#146, 157, 233, 318, 329, 342
Heaven / Eternal Life	#62, 96, 103, 148, 151, 191, 234, 236, 249, 262, 272, 293, 308, 321, 338
Honesty	#24, 59, 68, 172, 174, 282, 283, 297, 343
Hope	#118
Humility / All Sin	#1, 5, 39, 49, 60, 62, 75, 97, 100, 138, 146, 149, 178, 185, 187, 190, 201, 204, 206, 207, 243, 244, 278, 317, 347
Joy	#115, 256, 266, 267, 326
Knowledge / Understanding	#7, 14, 25, 26, 67, 94, 95, 112, 125, 162, 243, 256, 257, 258, 259, 280, 288, 294, 297, 298, 323, 324, 337
Life Eternal: See "Heaven"	
Limitations, Ours	17, 37, 94, 190, 271, 349

Love / Service	#139, 169, 329
Marriage / Family	#27, 29, 43, 44, 45, 51, 60, 83, 93, 107, 119, 123, 126, 192, 199, 222, 269, 307, 315, 344
Meaning to Life	#28, 31, 129, 329
Mortality	#58
Motivation	#12, 21, 181, 220, 323
Patriotism / Nation	#226
Parenting	#46, 47, 73, 89, 105, 110, 114, 140, 158, 212, 223, 251, 252, 273, 295, 312, 318, 319, 324
Patience	#32, 110, 111, 268
Persistence	#145, 183, 233, 241, 260
Possibilities / Power	#13, 80, 128, 139, 144, 190, 232, 237, 277, 278, 288, 289, 299, 302, 310, 333, 335
Prayer	#8, 9, 91, 191, 239, 246, 247, 248, 260, 303, 304
Preaching: See "Speaking"	
Prevenient Grace: See "Pursued by God"	
Pride	#2, 138, 161, 178, 270
Procrastination	#77, 78, 88
Providential Care	#42, 121, 124, 263, 310, 316, 335
Pursued by God	#300
Redemption	#86, 133, 137, 157, 179, 187, 202, 250
Repentance / Backsliding	#82, 102, 230, 250
Resurrection: See "Heaven / Life Eternal	
Rest	#122, 272
Security	#57
Self-worth	#142, 287
Senior Citizen	#66, 83, 209, 213, 275, 277, 308
Simplicity	#254
Sin / Mistakes	#33, 35, 40, 60, 61, 81, 95, 109, 194, 227
Solutions, Ours	#6, 74, 144, 218, 285, 317, 318
Speaking / Sermons	#169, 171, 177, 279, 313, 339
Surprises	#15
Surrender / Trust / Faith	263
Temptation	#4, 35, 36, 165, 202, 284
Thankfulness	#20, 124, 198, 238, 266
Treasure / Values	#115
Trials / Challenges	#23, 85, 127, 155, 159, 160, 167, 190, 191, 208, 214, 216, 228, 231, 270, 276, 292, 303, 306
Trust: See "Surrender"	
Truth	#297
Wake Up	#3
Witnessing	#41, 84, 87, 98, 135, 164, 184, 197, 271, 323, 325
Worship	#65
Worth: See "Self worth"	